CHASING
ACTUALITY

T.M. Sherman

Copyright © 2020 T.M. Sherman

All rights reserved.

Chasing Actuality is a work of fiction. The characters, places and events portrayed in this book are products of the author's imagination or are used fictiously. Any similarity to real persons, events, or places is coincidental.

Paperback ISBN: 9780692182017

PART 1

CHAPTER 1

"Come on, Chase, up you get. It's only 8:30 and I have a fabulous evening planned for us!"

I sighed, glanced at my watch, and promptly glared at Hayley for mobilizing me on my first free night in weeks. All I wanted to do was continue dozing on the couch with a hokey CGI-heavy action flick on in the background. But I could see I wasn't winning this battle, as she smirked back and held up the perfect peplum dress I had admittedly been dying to give a run for its money. It was one of those "just got my paycheck" purchases, which was an impulsive behavior I only sometimes engaged in.

So I felt obligated to put it to use. With that picture now stuck in my head, I sat up, reached out helplessly for the dress, and fifteen minutes later I was physically ready to go out, but my mind was still having trouble fully engaging.

"Why are you so quiet tonight?" Hayley asked.

"It's just been a long week at work, and honestly if you wanted to go dancing tonight you should have started feeding me alcohol and energy drinks hours ago." It was always fun to go out with Hayley, but it took an incredible amount of energy. And I wasn't exaggerating about work.

I was an evidence collections agent for a semi-clandestine international organization called the International Strategic Defense Agency, or ISDA, but it was more commonly known as "The Safe." The Safe was probably the most impenetrable organization that had ever existed, in all ways imaginable, or at least that was what they told us. Hayley and everyone else knew that I worked there, but they didn't know I was a field agent. I'd told them I was an analyst with a boring desk job.

That being said, it would've made no difference if I boasted to the world about how dangerous and thrilling my job was as an agent, but I wasn't allowed to tell anyone. And it was probably just because I wasn't allowed to that I wanted to so badly.

The Safe was so compartmentalized that even if someone tortured me and I told them everything I knew, it would've gotten them nowhere in terms of comprehensible intelligence. That's really the reason the past week (and most other weeks) had been so taxing, because it was hard enough just to get the necessary information for me to do my job before I could even begin the legwork. But like The Safe, I compartmentalized that frustration and finished getting ready for my girls' night out.

Hayley had ordered a car a few minutes ago, so we walked outside to wait. It was fairly brisk out so I would've preferred to wait inside, but these cars were impatient and usually only allowed for a thirty-second window to hop in. A minute or two later, a black coupe pulled up and we hopped inside.

"Please confirm rider code and destination," said a clearly-trying-not-to-be-monotonous disembodied voice.

"Hayley Marin, passenger 67804, destination Trader's Lounge."

"Ride confirmed. Have a nice journey." The driverless coupe lurched forward into a night that was seemingly full of promise.

I groaned. "You didn't tell me we were going to Traders. That place is a watering hole for pretentious techies with zero conversational skills. They don't even know how to buy girls drinks in there."

"What if I told you we didn't have to wait in line?" Hayley said, ignoring most of my reasons for protest.

"Yeah, okay," I replied, logic defeated.

We hopped out of the coupe and walked straight up to the bouncer. Hayley was as confident as ever, while I got carded per usual. I flipped on my E-ID from my watch and the bouncer waved us inside.

"How'd we get in?" I asked.

"We got in because you thought we were getting in. You'd be amazed at how far visualization and confidence can take you in life, lady." I almost wished we hadn't gotten in, just to ruin that awful mantra.

I followed her to the bar, and ordered my new usual gin and tonic. I must have been visibly annoyed at needing to flash my E-ID again, because Hayley made a comment about how I'd be grateful for looking like jailbait for years to come. Still no sign of that payoff.

We started making conversation with the bartender, who was really just a glorified host paid to make the clientele feel desirable, while a gimmicky robot behind the bar mixed our drinks.

"You ladies are in for a real treat tonight." He winked.

"Oh?" I looked up. "What's on tap?"

"I don't want to ruin the surprise, just make sure you're near the lounge area around 1:30."

My despair was audible. That was so far past my self-assigned bedtime. The "bartender" was actually pretty good at his job, though, and the night started to fly by. After an hour of drinking we started to dance, and after another hour we both lost interest and Hayley conveniently resurfaced and cut in.

Before long, the lights started to flicker dramatically. I walked over to the lounge. It looked like they had transformed the dancefloor into a pond full of dry ice. And then the main event appeared in the center of the mist.

"Ladies and gentlemen. As some of you may have heard, I've been popping into clubs around town to try out some of my latest tricks before my next show starts later this year..."

Hayley reappeared next to me, again conveniently, and turned pink. "No way!" She squealed in the most fangirl way. "That is *the* Smart Alec!"

What a terrible stage name, like laughably awful. But I was intrigued. Even those who refrained from Bay Area gossip columns knew that the magician Smart Alec had been indeed aweing club-goers around the bay area. This really wasn't fair, in my humble opinion, because a half—if not fully—intoxicated audience was hardly a good judge of the quality of an illusion.

I had most of my wits about me, though, and he did not disappoint. He did some very impressive sleight of hand and disappearing tricks, and some clever mentalism and mind-reading. He guessed the names, stories, and most intimate details of members of the crowd. I mean intimate literally, as he walked around describing the lacy lingerie that the ladies present were allegedly wearing. They swooned in confirmation, while I gagged a little. Then he sauntered over to us. "Hayley, right?"

Hayley gawked.

"Yes," I answered for her.

Alec winked at me and continued, "So, Miss Hayley. Would you like to play a game?" She nodded. "Have we ever met before?"

She found her voice and her composure. "No."

"What's your favorite color?"

"Purple."

"What's your spirit animal?"

"What? I don't know. Let's say a leopard."

Out of nowhere he whipped out a purple, leopard print scarf. "Good thing I know how to read women." The crowd laughed and applauded, and I was both slightly uncomfortable and amused.

He moved on to the next guest, and I took the opportunity to pay a visit to the ladies' room. When I returned, the lights had brightened and the crowd had dispersed. "You missed my finale," a voice whispered from behind me.

I whipped around and smiled. "Even magic can't win out over Mother Nature."

"I would have to disagree on that point, Chase," he said, bending what I assumed to be a trick spoon. "You can do anything if you set your mind to it."

Playfully, I grabbed the spoon out of his hand. I would've asked how he knew my name, but the point was moot. So I just continued smiling and playing up the drunk card.

"I'd say let's get a drink but I think it's past

last call," he continued. "Rain check?"

"I'd like that."

He somehow already had my number.

Monday morning I woke up feeling like I had wasted my entire weekend. I had spent half of Sunday in bed, and the other half nursing a hangover on the couch. My big accomplishment for the day was finishing the hokey action film, but it somehow lost most of its appeal when I had to balance unfairly loud sound effects with my massive headache. Such was life in your mid-twenties, and I now needed to jolt back to reality.

I glanced out the window as my train zoomed toward The Safe. The Safe was in the Middle of Nowhere, California, and I was fairly confident that this bullet train was crafted only for commuters in my very specific line of work under the guise of taxpayer funded high-speed travel. It was always ninety percent empty, so the internet was reliably fast and there were rarely any distractions. Needless to say, I took the opportunity to cyber stalk Smart Alec in peace.

There really wasn't much information available online before his magic career took off a year and a half ago. It was like he'd appeared out of thin air. I wasn't sure if that was ironic or the opposite of ironic.

"Good morning, Miss Silver," said the security bot at the front entrance to The Safe. I glanced up so the scanner could authenticate my retinas. "Your team is meeting in conference room A4 at 9:30 to discuss new intelligence that came in over the weekend."

I nodded and made my way through The Safe's labyrinth of offices and open workspaces toward my desk. I retracted my cube's walls and felt like stretching my legs before the meeting, so I activated treadmill mode while catching up on memos and emails from the weekend.

With nothing particularly interesting to respond to, I decided to head toward the conference room twenty minutes early. Our printouts were already on the table waiting for us. The two-page document was comprised primarily of computer jargon and an overwhelming number of ones and zeros. I'd learned to comprehend bits and pieces, but I really needed the tailored analysis to understand my role.

The document flashed yellow to signify medium urgency, so nothing to stress over yet. Other agents trickled in, some with too-warm-for-Monday greetings and others looking stern. Brooke Jameson took the seat to my right. The girl was brilliant and I considered myself lucky that she always chose to partner with me on field ops, but it was like she went through the motions of wanting to be the best of friends but was completely impassive when it came down to it.

Brooke was incredibly passionate about her job and the agency, and external relationships just seemed to be a lot further down on her priority list. But she was always amicable and easy to get along with. "Looks like Sid had a busy weekend," she muttered, reading through the jargon much more expertly than myself.

There were a few rumors about how Sid had gotten his name.

At one point, Brooke and I posited that he was a modern-day Siddhartha, the founder of Buddhism. While Brooke had expressed her belief that Sid would eventually bring about world peace, I viewed him more as a self-declared god—albeit a benevolent one—with an authoritarian power over the people.

And I wasn't even a skeptic, just a realist. The skeptics associated Sid with the demonic child in the Disney classic *Toy Story*, who enjoyed experimenting on toys he thought couldn't fight back.

Sid actually stood for Security Information Display. Not very flashy, but what everyone did agree on was that Sid was incredible in the truest sense of the word. It was hard to believe he actually existed.

What Sid was, in fact, was an incredibly advanced artificial intelligence algorithm that could calculate every single little thing. Like really little. He was omniscient, building an infinite number of models based on all of the digital information and recorded history available. He boiled every thought down to electric impulses, with predictable chemical reactions, and therefore predictable actions.

This was the example that had been provided for me: Say I had plans to meet a friend for dinner at the new French place that just opened up down the street at 7:30 pm on a Friday. Based on my digital footprint history, Sid would predict that I would leave work at 5:20. He would also predict the times that everyone else would be leaving work and would be getting on the road, the routes they would take based on GPS navigation, and that it would take me until 6:15 to get home.

He would then assume, based on my historical tastes and preferences, which outfit I would decide on and how long it would take me to get ready, and was doing the same calculation for everyone else, simultaneously. So, Sid would know there was an incredibly high likelihood that by the time I got to the French restaurant there would be a 45-minute wait, one that I would not be willing to commit to. Sid would also connect the fact that the billboard for takeout sushi down the street would catch my eye and I'd end up getting carryout from there and taking it home.

So Sid would tell me in the morning just to go straight for the sushi, saving me the would-be headache.

The Safe had narrowed down the type of

activity that Sid looked out for, however, and he was strictly reserved for international security purposes. Sid spat out corresponding intelligence that he based predictions on for matters of international security. Then agents like myself went out to collect evidence to back up Sid's predictions.

"Brooke, how was your weekend?"

Darren Waddell had just entered the room with his smug swagger, rudely awakening me from my reverie. "Lovely. Thanks, Darren," she replied. They talked through their time off while I turned my attention to my report. Darren had made it very clear that he thought I was too young and way out of my element being here, but Brooke kept him at bay.

Eventually our handler, Caleb Harris, entered the room. "Happy Monday, ladies and gents," he said, looking anything but happy. "Secretary Fuller is out sick today. Would one of you like to volunteer to take over her duties for the time being?"

Brooke's hand shot into the air. Fuller was far from just a secretary; she had access to secure files far beyond our pay grade. And it wasn't like we could bring in an outside temp. Naturally the fill-in would only have "need to know" access, but it was still an exciting opportunity for Brooke at least. Supervisor Harris approved of and thanked Brooke for volunteering.

"That means you will be flying solo today,

Agent Silver. Are you alright with that?"

He genuinely wanted to know, because it was against the agency's strictest policies for agents to be out of their comfort zones in the field. I thought it over—it would be a first for me. "Yes, that's fine for today," I replied coolly.

"Great, then let's begin the debrief. Sid thought it prudent to alert us of an impending display of foreign aggression near our international headquarters. You have all been assigned a separate event to photograph or documents to collect before we can move forward," Harris said, vague as always. We were never told more than a fraction of the full story for fear of a mole or security breach.

"Agents, please come collect your individual assignments... Dalton, Gregorio, Mills." Eventually, he arrived at "s." "Silver."

I approached his tablet and entered my 18-digit passcode that changed every month. It sent a digital copy of my assignment to my tablet, and I quickly opened up the new document:

> *Attention: Agent Chase M. Silver*
> *March 3rd, 2122*
> <u>*Assignment:*</u>
> *Please make your way toward coordinates [1.2814801 103.85274800000002 13.2025032122]. Upon arrival, photograph interaction in its entirety between subject A, wearing jeans and a yellow and black plaid button-down shirt, and subject B, wearing a*

*long black skirt and cream blazer. Please col-
lect and use alias 17D. Your utmost discretion is encouraged.*
Signed, Director Chambers

I wonder if she actually signs off on all of these, I thought offhandedly to myself. Well, this would be an easy journey. I immediately recognized those coordinates as being located in Singapore, home of Safe International Headquarters and my favorite destination in the field.

Knowing full well that we never had much time to spare once receiving an assignment, I nodded goodbye to those team members still in the meeting room and took off toward the locker room to grab my field kit. I needed to do a quick but thorough check to make sure everything was in order.

I thumbed through the kit, complete with local currency, my contact lens camcorder or "camtact" as I liked to call it, the corresponding remote concealed in my lip gloss vial, a satellite phone, nutritional goo (for long stakeouts), 17D alias identification, and an extra GPS tracker. I threw in my nearly invisible stun gun and opened my new passport. I was now Debbie Kay from Easterly Territory, one of the newest independent states of the Americas, and it was time I got into character.

Adopting a new disguise and persona was usually my favorite part of any mission. A bit juvenile for me to enjoy it so much, I'll admit, but the novelty of this kind of dress up had yet to get old for me. The number coordinated with the outfit, so I was looking for wardrobe 17 on the other side of the locker room.

I slid open the appropriate locker and pulled out my goodies: a very stylish off-white pant-length jumpsuit, lightly heeled sandals, a chestnut long bob of a wig, and a beautifully embroidered handbag. Simple, yet elegant enough to blend into the fashion mecca that was Singapore. I slipped into the romper and expertly concealed my long blonde ponytail under my new brunette hairdo.

Admiring my new look in the mirror, I considered the persona component. I had been assigned 17D, and D was a bit more complex than your standard personality and backstory. Debbie was a high-end art consultant, with a Southern twang. She could switch from being the center of attention at an art auction to an invisible gallery observer at the flip of a switch. Debbie was divorced and bitter, with an unquenchable thirst to be more successful than her ex-husband. I was not really sure why any of this was necessary for snapping a few discreet photos, but alias prep was always mandatory.

So the lovely divorcee Debbie Downer grabbed her embroidered bag, now full of spy supplies, and speed-walked down to the loops.

Miles and miles beneath the agency, a complex network of restricted hyperloops sprawled out under the earth's surface. Public hyperloops were easily the most efficient mode of mass transit today, but even those moved at a snail's pace when compared with these beauties.

We currently had about 3,000 destinations, and it seemed like more were being added each day. I was pretty sure our capsules could rival the speed of light, that's how fast they are. This loop system, and Sid of course, were two of the agency's most closely held secrets.

I had a very primitive understanding of the physics behind it. All I knew was that I entered my coordinates into the lift, the lift took me to the corresponding capsule, and I lay down inside and glided effortlessly through a vacuum while suspended in midair by some very impressive magnets. And with such incomprehensible speeds at our disposal, we could be anywhere in the world within minutes.

After again confirming my coordinates, the capsule popped open for me to load myself in. I put my shoes and handbag into the designated bin next to my seat and buckled in. "Agent Silver, please confirm your return coordinates before departing," said a disembodied voice from above. I muttered them from memory, adjusting the last few digits for this specific tube. "Thank you, Agent. Have a safe journey."

The lights dimmed and I closed my eyes. They kept it dark so you weren't thrown off by how quickly you accelerated, but I chose to shut my eyes so I could visualize the motion and enjoy the rush. The backrest lowered down so I was roughly at a thirty-degree angle, with my bare feet dangling above the ground. I heard the final locks click into place and the countdown begin. "5...4...3...2...1..." And with that, I barely felt the acceleration, like I was weightless, gliding through space and time.

It was blissful, and the eight-and-a-half-minute journey was over much too quickly. The seat returned to its original upright position, and after slipping my sandals and bag back on, I left the capsule and took the lift up to greet the rest of my workday in the wondrous place that was Singapore.

The lift brought me up to B2, or two levels underground, so I couldn't say exactly where the exit point was or how deep I had been. While Singapore was decades ahead of its time in terms of city planning, architecture, and overall aesthetics, its true awesomeness lay miles under the surface—and I'm not just talking about the hyperloop network.

Singapore had literally built underground skyscrapers, or floor scrapers, as they were perhaps more aptly called, that included routine businesses, manufacturing centers, defense initiatives, and storage warehouses. This city could've thrived in isolation for a century just based on its reserves—with its highways, railways, and artificial sunlight—so that no one really ever had to come up to the surface for air.

The underground indeed took care of all the city's *needs*, which left everything above ground for the city's *wants*. The land of grand beauty and leisure emerged around me as I finally exited another lift above ground, my view immediately obstructed by the iconic boat hotel, Marina Bay Sands. Ancient by Singapore standards, everyone had seen pictures of this structure that looked like a massive boat suspended by three towers that was covered by constantly changing holographic displays on the tower's panels.

The panels were advertising an Asian rom com, where the humor in the preview had definitely been lost in translation. This hotel used to be a stone's throw from the ocean, by Safe International Headquarters. But Singapore had taken the dirt from the excavation of the underground city and literally expanded the country with the dug up earth.

They'd named it "reclaimed land," but it was so much more than a physical expansion; it was an offensive strategy. Singapore's government wanted to expand as far as possible into the South China Sea, which was one of the key reasons The Safe had been founded, and why we were also ensured ocean-front property.

I wasn't headed to headquarters, though, but to the country's nearest Mass Rapid Transit (MRT) station. I needed to get to the tech epicenter, "One-North," via the Yellow Line, or rather a coffee shop adjacent to the tech epicenter that served as my rendezvous point.

After exiting the MRT, I ducked into the bathroom and inserted my camtacts (normal contacts to the naked eye, with a 4K camera lens in the middle that casually lay atop the retina). I just needed to insert them and press the remote, concealed as my lip gloss, in order to take the pictures. All I had left to do was find the cafe, a spot with a good vantage point, and wait.

In full Debbie mode, I waltzed into the coffee shop at the appropriate coordinates. It looked like a converted shop house, with a hodgepodge of nostalgic entertainment plastered to the walls. Printed newspapers and DVD covers littered the tables. Some might've called it artsy, but I saw it as a subpar attempt to attract the huppies, or hipster-yuppies. Really one and the same these days.

The cafe was bustling, mostly with to-go orders, so I was able to snag a table next to the window. I ordered a flat white, pulled out my book on late 21st century architecture, and settled down. And I didn't have to wait long, thanks to Sid's immaculate calculations.

Not even three minutes after sitting down, the man in the yellow and black plaid button-down and a highly composed lady in a cream blazer walked in. I didn't know their names or backstories, or what they knew or were supposedly capable of. I was just there to blindly collect evidence of this meeting, and so I did.

I hit the subtle "Record" button on my lip gloss remote, and watched. Then I slumped in my seat with a dazed look on my face so the other patrons wouldn't take notice. The two chatted and laughed carelessly, not exactly having a serious meeting. Thirty minutes passed without much action. The most interesting thing that happened was when the man's hand slipped and subtly grazed the woman's knuckles.

She shivered ever so slightly at his touch and her lovely set of bangles on her otherwise bare wrist clinked. I wasn't surprised though; he was a really good-looking guy.

They both glanced down at their phones, and it looked like they were figuring out another time to meet up. They seemed to agree on a later date, pecked each other on the cheek, and exited the cafe. I slowly looked around to make sure my camtacts would capture the full 360-degree setting, then stopped recording. I twisted the lip gloss so it would automatically upload my footage to a highly secure cloud-based server that I could access later.

The top of the lip gloss gave a barely audible pop, so I knew the footage was safely stored and I could now return back home. This had been a very normal collection mission, but I still felt that slight sense of relief knowing it had gone smoothly.

As my gut relaxed, I realized it was well past lunchtime and I had a very immediate need for food.

From what I'd read, Singapore used to have an abundance of cheap, delicious Asian specialties from around the region. They used to be called "hawker centers" and were a staple of the city-state's culture. Today, there were a few of these that had been preserved, but I got the sense that they were not true to their ancestors' version. There was no aroma of grease or angry elderly women barking at you for your order as I'd read about in the history briefs. It was all very pleasant and sterile.

I visited one not too far from the cafe and looked at the pictures of food to choose from. The prices, at least, were certainly not what they used to be. I pointed to a picture of a noodle dish with an egg and chicken. It looked tasty enough, but most importantly I could decipher the ingredients from the picture. I'd learned the importance of paying attention to pictures; otherwise you might just end up with a full fish head in your dish, eyeballs and all.

That happened to me once, and since then, everything I'd tried here had tasted a little bit fishy. But this noodle dish was solid, and after eating and feeling a little bit more content with my latest Singaporean exploration, I made my way back to the loops.

CHAPTER 2

Alas, something in the noodles definitely did not agree with me. As soon as I made it back to The Safe, I had a fun-filled trip to the ladies' room and promptly hopped on the train to go home. When I returned to my sparsely decorated, but arguably intentionally minimalistic one-bedroom apartment, I was so grateful for the quiet. I curled up on the couch around dusk and woke up startled around 4 am. I'm one of those people who, if I hear any sort of noise or sense any movement, no matter how deep my slumber, I'll be fully alert within milliseconds.

I jumped off the couch and did a thorough check around the apartment, not sure what had startled me. None of the doors or windows appeared to have been opened, and all was quiet. It was times like these when for a fleeting instant I wished I didn't live alone. Still a bit spooked and not wanting to shut off the lights, I cut my losses and decided to get ready for the day. I had a good amount of time to spare before catching my train, so I decided to check out one of those early morning workout raves. These breakfast raves, or *braves*, had been on my bucket list for a while.

"Would you like a green life smoothie sample?" some unabashed huppy wearing expensive workout clothes asked me as I entered.

I nodded, and then paused. "Are there any drugs in it?"

She feigned offense and turned toward the next group coming into the warehouse. I assumed that meant no to the drug question, but I couldn't be sure, so I ditched the smoothie.

The warehouse was drafty and smelled of cold sweat, not the most inviting of aromas. But I was still curious, so I continued past some people in varying levels of yoga stances and massage circles through the entryway and into the main dance room.

Now this finally looked fun. People were packed like sardines, just jumping around and dancing to, well, dance music, without a care in the world. And not in an uncomfortable, dirty grinding way. Pretty much everyone was dancing as if they were in the center of a mosh pit just having a blast by themselves. It only took a few seconds before I felt comfortable joining in, dancing contentedly, and quite badly at that. But I was burning calories so it was fine.

I felt a familiar tap on my shoulder. "Fancy seeing you here, Miss Silver."

I smiled to myself before turning around. "You know if you could make my sweat disappear so I looked presentable, I'd be sincerely impressed." I could feel the magician's eyes smile back. I knew it was him even before I saw his face.

"Chase, I know this is confusing, but just do me a favor and try to look like you're still having an unapologetic blast dancing while I explain." I complied and continued moving to the music. "Listen, you're going to have a lot of questions. I know that. But you of all people should know there's a reason for the information you're given and that you should respect the process."

My head started spinning. *Does Alec work at The Safe? Is this part of a mission? Is that the only reason he was flirting with me at the club?*

He continued, "You're not supposed to know about me, and it's of the utmost importance that no one finds out you do right now. But I need your help. There's a problem with the photos you brought back yesterday. Please go through them again and let me know when you find it. You'll be able to find me when you need me."

And just like that he was gone.

Thoroughly bewildered, I left the dance floor and went back to my apartment to shower and get ready for the day. Questions were indeed racing through my mind and I started working backwards. Maybe Alec had made a loud noise outside my window, waking me up and getting me to the noisy dance club where his actions and intentions would remain unknown. That's what I would have done if I wanted to set up a covert meeting. But why, what was the problem? What information was in the pictures? What was Alec's relationship to The Safe?

For some reason that I hoped I wouldn't regret later, I trusted him and his unknown motives. I boarded the train like nothing strange had happened and continued to act as such throughout the day. I went back through my files and opened the photos I had taken yesterday.

Brooke quietly entered the room. "Chase! What are you doing here?"

I started to stammer a reply, trying to figure out a cover before I realized I wasn't doing anything unusual. "What? What do you mean?"

"I heard you went home sick yesterday after your trip. How are you feeling?" she asked sincerely.

"Oh right, I'm much better. I pretty much fell asleep as soon as I got back and that made a huge difference. I feel like a new woman. A woman who has full control over the contents of her stomach." Okay, that was a little too much information, but she definitely wasn't going to question me after that.

"Well, I'm so glad you're feeling better. I felt so awful that of all days to leave you on your own, I chose yesterday! I could have steered you away from whatever you ate that gave you that bug."

"You're sweet, but honestly it's no big deal. Everyone gets food poisoning when they're on a mission. At least it was Singapore and not one of the neighboring countries. Then I might have been out of commission for weeks." I smiled. She returned my smile and went back to work.

I started flipping through the photos once again and all seemed in order. I had no clue what I was supposed to be looking for, and whatever it was, it certainly wasn't obvious. It was just a normal coffee date between two good-looking, impeccably well-dressed people. I sat there staring for hours before I figured it out.

Yesterday, I could have sworn that the woman did not have a tattoo on her wrist. Bangles yes, but tattoo—no. I was one hundred percent certain. But today, there was an almost imperceptible butterfly tattoo on the underside of her forearm. *That is really, really strange*, I thought to myself.

To say I was intrigued would be an understatement, but how did one begin to research something like this? The Safe had its own extensive internal knowledge base, but looking up "inconsistency in imagery" or "photo changing after one day" seemed like it might be a red flag down the road, so I wanted to tread with caution here.

We also had the tools to identify the people in the photo and I could look more into *their* backstories, but that was entirely against protocol. Even if I could anonymize my query, which I probably couldn't do anyway, it would be pretty obvious it was me who was interested in learning more about them, since I was the one who took the photo of them in the first place. Naturally, this would be entirely against The Safe's mainstay of compartmentalization.

Ignoring this inconsistency simply wasn't an option, though I couldn't say exactly why. It was a bit of unfortunate irony that I had all the tools at my disposal, but couldn't utilize them to do my research unless I wanted to be tracked. Considering my boss's boss was an omni-present and omni-potent computer, this research project needed to be planned and executed with utmost caution and discretion.

Looking up anything online would be difficult. I thought about going to the library and logging in from a public computer, but you still needed to login for access through your E-ID. It was practically impossible to surf the web anonymously, which I normally thought was a great thing for accountability and security. But now this was proving to be an incredible nuisance, and for once I empathized with the Internet Freedom Fighters (a prominent digital privacy rights activist group).

I briefly toyed with the idea of purchasing a false E-ID identity on the dark web, but I wasn't entirely confident that I had the technical aptitude to do so. The dark web had been driven even further underground, metaphorically speaking, than the loops. I also knew The Safe had set up fake seller accounts to trap those with nefarious intent—which was probably more of a deterrent than anything, but still didn't want to risk it.

After ruling out the dark web as an option, I

realized that I was limited to hard copies or verbal communication. That evening after work, I found myself venturing into the history section of an antique bookstore. Of course, there wasn't a book about the innerworkings of The Safe, so without much to go on, I opted for *The Beginning: Strategic Interests and the Evolution of Homeland Security*.

The Safe was version 10.0 of the Department of Homeland Security, which had ended up far outranking other security-related departments like the FBI and CIA on the totem pole. I found a chapter labeled "An Introduction to AI-Powered Security" and jumped ahead.

> *It soon became obvious that the computing power of machines had become intelligent enough to analyze emerging situations, especially those that escalated to hostile or violent levels, better than human operatives. There was one key turning point when the DHS set up two identical training environments. These environments were modeled after a real event, a horrific bombing at a supermarket in Latin America.*
>
> *The circumstances surrounding the bombing maintained a "Top Secret" classification, and very few people knew exactly what happened. Yet these training environments recreated the scene with exact detail, and one of the high-*

est-ranking intelligence officers was tasked with analyzing the situation and following a corresponding course of action to prevent the bombing. A computer was given the same task. The operative would have theoretically perished if the training "bomb" was real, and the computer—if it had legs—would have walked out unscathed. The rest was history.

This was the backstory of how Sid came to be. He calculated an infinite number of scenarios based on variations in even the smallest detail, and correctly predicted the course of action that would not result in bloodshed. The hairs on the back of my neck stood up, which I instinctively knew was a pretty good indication that I was on the right track. But I still had a long way to go before solving the inconsistent picture predicament.

That event had triggered a massive schism between national security hawks and advocates for privacy and freedom. The latter cried out against the potential ramifications of AI-powered "pre-crime," a science fiction theme that now posed a real moral question—"If you know what's going to happen, should you take the necessary measures to stop it?"

During the early days of Sid, the freedom fighters won. The US government could not use this new technology to act on upcoming events within its borders. Which was precisely why The Safe was created clandestinely: to use this technology to proactively take action on upcoming events overseas.

They didn't actually go over that murky historical justification during your training at The Safe, but it was something I'd picked up on over the years. I thought about the picture again, and that missing butterfly tattoo.

Perhaps it wasn't a tattoo at all.

CHAPTER 3

Maybe someone had drawn a butterfly on the image I had been looking at to send a signal. I needed to look at the photo again in order to confirm my suspicion about there being an extra layer of ink, but that had to be the answer. At that point, the meaning came easily to me. My immediate interpretation was that the butterfly was representative of the butterfly effect. My thoughts spiraled.

The butterfly effect, of course, was the widely known idea that one small change in events could completely transform the course of the future. Someone clearly wanted to warn against the effects of changing fate, which was exactly what Sid was doing. We were all familiar with this argument and supporters of this argument. Even within the innermost circles that knew about Sid, Sid was an extremely controversial technological innovation. But I believed that Sid's analytical and predictive prowess was now just part of the definition of "fate," if there was such a thing.

So I got the message, and it wasn't anything earth shattering. The cause for my concern was now about how someone had gotten access to the photos. Did we have a mole in my department? And who could I trust to discuss the situation in confidence?

I had no idea, because while I had acquaintances at work, I couldn't immediately rule out anyone. I needed to find Alec. He clearly had an associate he wanted me to know about.

Even though my previous search to dig into Alec's past had proven futile, I had some better ideas for digging into his present. He had quite a fan following these days, and no one could make a pervasive hashtag disappear. I took to social media, swallowed my pride as I searched #smartalec, and shortly thereafter knew exactly where to find him.

Luckily, I didn't have to go back to the breakfast rave.

It was one of those rare, perfect spring days in the city, and it was hardly even frowned upon to call in sick when it hit sunny and 75 degrees. Normally I wouldn't have dreamed of playing hooky, especially considering the recent sick day I had just taken, but I felt I had no choice other than to join the masses and flock to a nearby park. Knowing without a doubt that she would be at the "scene," I messaged Hayley to meet up and she promptly responded with her GPS location and a "jumping for joy" emoji.

My assumption was correct—she was at the same park where someone had just spotted

"Smart Alec" per his associated hashtag. I immediately posted a pic of Hayley and myself upon arrival to avoid suspicion into my true motives. I made sure to include the playground behind us in the photo so that our location was easily identifiable.

Brooke almost immediately commented that she was jealous and wished she had gotten the invite. So there was no doubt that she'd relay my activity to our superiors at The Safe, which was fine as I felt I had built up enough trust and goodwill that they'd have no problem with me taking some personal time.

Before long, I saw Alec leaning against a nearby tree. "Grabbing some water," I told Hayley. "I'll catch up with you later."

"Okay, I'll be around."

As I started to approach Alec, he turned away and began walking at a leisurely pace. I took that to mean that I should follow.

After a few twists and turns, we ended up in a crowded alleyway with giant murals spanning hundreds of feet along the wall. Tourists and locals alike were admiring the artwork, allowing Alec and me to blend in easily.

"Ah, Miss Silver. Fancy seeing you here." He smiled at me.

A little disarmed, I told him, "I understood your message."

He nodded. "You're a quick study. You must have so many questions."

"Just one main one," I said. "Who is the mole?"

Alec looked quizzical. "What mole?"

"Well, I'm not sure if he or she is an associate of yours, or if you are just aware that there is a breach. I'm assuming that's why you pointed out the photo with the new butterfly 'tattoo?' Clearly, someone on the inside of The Safe had access to draw it on the photo." He didn't say anything to that, so I somewhat nervously continued on. I wasn't good with awkward silences.

"Look, I know there are a lot of critics when it comes to what we do at The Safe, that our computing power is changing the future quite literally. I have my reasons for why I'm okay with this and I'm happy to have an ethical debate with you at a later date. But right now I need to address the breach, and I'm not entirely sure why, but I'd like to do so without implicating you."

I thought he would be happy about that, but he suddenly had a stern look on his face. All he responded with was, "I think you missed the point."

He started to turn and walk away, and I felt desperate—an emotion that I was completely unfamiliar with. He sped up, and I followed. Leaving fifteen feet between the two of us, I followed him for what felt like miles. We ended up in a seedier part of town, where he abruptly stopped.

"Are you ready to go down the rabbit hole?" Despite my mental hesitation, my body left me no choice. I'd unwittingly follow him anywhere.

I recognized the neighborhood as north of Civic Center, and we ducked into a dark alley. "We have to time this right," he said. "Be ready to jump."

Having no idea what he was talking about, I simply nodded. About a hundred feet from where we stood sat a ramp that was perpendicular to the alley. I heard movement in the distance and wondered if we were about to have company. Before long, a biker appeared but didn't seem to be turning down the alley, so I didn't think anything of it. The bike continued along the elevated ramp, and just then Alec hissed from a distance, "Chase, jump forward NOW."

Looking down to see where his voice was coming from, I realized that I had somehow completely missed him removing a manhole cover and jumping into it. It must have only taken him a second, and I couldn't make myself jump without knowing where I would land.

I understood the urgency, though, and the best I could do was take a small step forward. That was enough. I plummeted down about ten feet onto some sort of padded surface. The manhole cover had already resealed our entrance.

"This is one of the few places left in the world that Sid doesn't know about," Alec began. "It's a tunnel from World War II that was obscured from historical records. Some sympathetic Americans used this to transport Japanese Americans to safety from the internment camps." I was about to respond that I had never heard that story, but of course that was obvious. If Sid didn't know about it, no one did.

Not knowing what to say next, I just asked, "Well, how do you know about it?"

"Ironically, direct word of mouth is the only reliable form of communication these days. Wires can get crossed or compromised. We've had to revert back to our most primitive form of conversing," he said almost bitterly. "My distant relatives were those 'sympathetic Americans,' so they passed the whereabouts of these tunnels down my family line."

"So being a rebel is in your blood," I half-joked.

"I prefer protector or seeker of justice." He smiled loftily.

"That's almost as cheesy as your name, Mr. Smart Alec."

"How long have you been waiting to say that?" He paused. "I don't smile genuinely very often these days, so thank you for that, Miss Silver." I hoped he felt the undeniable chemistry that I was so drawn to, but we clearly had some other business to address first.

"So to sum up," he continued, "you believe that someone on the inside of The Safe manually edited the photo to include the butterfly tattoo, as some sort of signal about the butterfly effect? And that I have sought you out to connect you with this person with the hope of turning you against The Safe and everything it stands for? Is that accurate?"

"Well, yes, I suppose so," I stammered. It did sound pretty juvenile when he phrased it that way. "What else was I supposed to take away from your cryptic signals?"

"Just enough to get you here, so I guess it worked," he replied. "Sid makes things complicated. I couldn't outright ask you to meet me or take you by force because that computer would know. It had to be subtle clues that just counted on your intuition. Flirting with you at the bar to get you interested enough to listen, giving you the clue at that awful breakfast dance party. Both were crowded enough places to not attract attention, letting your mind lead you down this path on its own...not that the flirting wasn't authentic," he quickly added.

I couldn't help but feel a bit annoyed, but his rationale made sense. The butterfly tattoo still didn't add up though. "While that is all logical, the butterfly is not. You didn't have me do that research for nothing, so if it's not a manual edit then you need to start explaining. And how do you know so much about Sid and The Safe anyway?"

"Follow me." He started to walk down the tunnel. "We can walk and talk. As I mentioned earlier, this tunnel has been obscured from historical record since World War II. Now, you probably were taught that the technology behind Sid emerged with the South American bombing catastrophe, but in reality, the technology had already been in the works for more than half a century. This tunnel is proof, and my family had a big part to play in it."

I sighed. I knew all about the conspiracies surrounding Alan Turing and his infamous test. It was widely accepted that Turing had created a test after World War II that could determine whether a machine was as intelligent as a human. But conspiracy theorists alleged that Turing actually created the framework for Sid, and the triumphs of MI-6 during the war were much further entrenched in artificial intelligence than what the history books told us. They suggested the famed Enigma decryption center set up by Britain to decrypt messages sent by the Nazis was really the earliest form of advanced artificial intelligence. This was "obscured" from the history books because the US wanted credit for such an achievement. And so on and so forth.

"This has nothing to do with Turing," said Alec, reading my mind. I had to remember that he was a magician after all.

CHAPTER 4

"My family wasn't MI-6. They were actually Austrian. Are you familiar with the story of Schrödinger's cat?"

"Familiar might be an overstatement," I replied.

"Well, one of my ancestors worked closely with a physicist named Erwin Schrödinger for many years. They worked deeply in quantum mechanics, and the cat story centers around a thought experiment about different realities that coexist. An oversimplified explanation is that if you poison a cat in a box, it might be alive or it might be dead until it is observed one way or another. As soon as someone opens the box, that reality prevails."

I scratched the side of my head. Alec must've sensed my confusion, because he continued, "The rationale isn't the important part, because as I said it's really an oversimplification. I don't understand the math myself. My relative wasn't satisfied with the premise, however, and continued to explore. He essentially believed that the cat would continue to exist as both dead and alive in separate realities. That the experiment would apply to separate branches of the universe that could not touch each other. That there are an infinite number of branches and many versions—sometimes identical or very different—from the world that you and I live in.

"Under this premise, all possible past events that led to differing futures are real. The theoretical analysis of this idea continued to deepen and stay in the philosophical realm in Western Europe during the decades following World War II. My family, though, had long since left for the United States. They tried a more practical application of what we know now as the multiverse hypothesis."

My eyes widened; he really had my attention now. "Well, if you figured out how to jump back and forth between worlds," I interrupted, "then it explains why you're such a good magician. Your awe-inspiring magic show stunts must be child's play." Still skeptical, my instinct was always to lighten the mood, which in this case was probably a defense mechanism for a significant mental overload.

"The magic act is just a means to an end," he said with a shrug. We abruptly came to a halt in front of what seemed like a concrete wall, but it was pitch black so it was a little difficult to fully make out. He asked me, "What do you see?"

"A very hard wall," I replied, tilting my head sideways in anticipation.

"Now, what if I told you what is in front of

you confuses the brain so much that it can't process what you are looking at, and there is something quite different in front of you?"

"Then I'd tell you to prove it."

He took out two images from his pocket and shined the light from his phone on both. "Tell me what you see."

"One shows a white chess set against a black background, and the other shows a black chess set against a white background," I said.

He proceeded to take out a pocketknife and cut out one black and one white chess piece. He held them up to each other. "Which is which?" he asked. They were indistinguishable.

"Nice optical illusion," I said, thinly veiling my actual surprise. "But I don't see where you're going with this."

"Think about observation and perception here. Your view of the colors is subject to the background they are up against. The chess pieces look different when placed in front of contrasting colors, even though they are objectively the same.

In this scenario, you are very used to looking at matter. It makes up everything around you. He extinguished his light. Because there is an absolute absence of light in this tunnel, what lies in front of you is the precise opposite. This is what we call dark matter. Normally it is not visible to the naked eye—you need to know where and how to look."

"So, we're looking at dark matter that you

happened to stumble upon?"

"More or less. Dark matter makes up the majority of the universe, so it's all around us—it's just not normally accessible. When you happen upon dark matter in this way, it can serve as a portal in between these oftentimes indistinguishable universes. You jumped into another universe when you went through that manhole, and this 'wall' ahead of us, as you called it, allows us to explore.

"These tunnels were used, as I mentioned, as a method of safe transport. But the real reason you haven't read reports on them is because they do not exist in the universe we know."

This was a lot to swallow.

"So why don't people fall or walk between universes all the time then?" I asked, raising an eyebrow.

"Most dark matter is found in smaller units, if you will. It's rare that you find a block big enough to walk through. It does happen, though. Sometimes people will walk through to a universe that is almost indistinguishable from their own and never realize. Some people do realize, and either seem crazy to the rest of their discovered world or actually go crazy trying to find their way back."

"In the universe that we are currently in, could I theoretically run into another 'me'?" This was an unsettling thought.

"Theoretically, yes. I am not aware of this happening, though. I'm not sure why. I just have a theory."

"Elaborate."

"We know that when matter and *antimatter* meet, not to be confused with dark matter, an incredible amount of energy is released and annihilation occurs. I believe the same thing would happen when a person met his or her alternate universe counterpart. They would both cease to exist."

Well, that's unfortunate, I thought to myself. Reading my expression, he steered the discussion elsewhere.

"I know this is a lot to take in, and even if you understand it conceptually, it's still hard to wrap your mind around. Theoretical physics is no walk in the park. I barely understand it myself. What I want to bring to your attention, though, is how this relates to The Safe and Sid."

I nodded in response.

"The reason why Sid is so powerful, so omniscient, is that Sid is able to weave electromagnetic waves in and out of the multiverse, essentially connecting to 'Sids' in other worlds, infinitely magnifying the computing power. This is how Sid is able to assess all possible outcomes of a scenario and suggest a corresponding action with such a high degree of accuracy. Each scenario is actually happening in at least one of these other worlds." He seemed to have one more seemingly uncomfortable thing to say.

"The butterfly tattoo that you thought was

drawn on the photo was actually the woman's tattoo in another world."

Of all the crazy things Alec had just relayed to me, this last sentiment was the one that hit home. I gawked, realizing that the woman in the photo was not the same woman I had taken a photo of in Singapore. It begged the question, who was the other photographer? How did the photos get switched?

"What I don't understand is why you are telling me all this," I said, shaking my head slowly. "Why you sought me out. It seems like all the ethical questions remain the same. Should a computer have the power to create a carefully calculated future for the welfare of the people? I don't care how many computers we're talking about—it still seems like a good thing to me. We live in a safer, happier world."

"Yes, but at what cost?"

A realization suddenly hit me. "The hyperloops!" I exclaimed. "Every time I've gone on a mission, I've been transported to a different universe through tunnels like these, haven't I?"

He nodded. "Precisely. Except this tunnel was created by people in this alternate world to serve a purpose and provide refuge in a time of need. It allowed prisoners to escape and go on to lead fruitful lives. My family was lucky they found it and were able to explore its meaning further. Sid, on the other hand, is more or less creating these tunnels. The computer has an unfair advantage now, dictating the fate not just of our world, but the multiverse. It's too much consolidated power, and it has to be stopped."

"You're right. This is a lot to take in," I said after a minute, stroking my chin deep in thought. But my data-driven nature took hold. "Can you provide some specific examples of what you consider to be Sid's abuse of power?"

"Sure. I'll provide two particularly relevant examples. The first is quite expansive. Do you know why most of today's politicians, regardless of party affiliation, are so hawkish? It's not necessarily what the people want, but they are the best men and women to ensure security as a top priority. Hence, Sid has calculated all the scenarios to get these people into office. He's essentially been fixing elections since his inception. Goodbye to any semblance of democracy." His voice was flat.

"I never thought about it that way," I admitted, twisting my mouth. But deep down I had known. I just had so truly believed in protecting the world at large. Then, Alec's tone changed to something very, well, soft.

"Now I'll get to the second example momentarily, but first, do you have an older sister?" That came out of nowhere, and immediately sent shivers down my spine.

"Yes, well, I did... She passed away nearly a decade ago." Tears sprung to my eyes of their own accord. I blinked hard to fight them back. "Why bring that up?"

"I hate to press you on this, but how did she die?" he asked, in a very sensitive, compassionate way.

"A domestic terrorism attack—a bombing during her last year at university. It was horrible. We went to the same school, and I happened to be off-site interviewing for internships at the time. She was just in the wrong place at the wrong time. There were only four fatalities that day, and while I'd wish that tragedy on no one, I still don't understand why it had to be her. She was my best friend."

"I can't even imagine how hard that must have been for you." He patted me soothingly on the back. "Now, not to be cavalier, but you were majoring in creative writing at the time, weren't you?"

"Yes, I loved to write back then. But I was so distraught after the bombing I dropped out of all my writing electives. I was still able to graduate with a liberal arts degree, but I haven't been able to put pen to paper since."

"Well, what if I told you that in at least one other reality, your sister is alive and you've already written two best-sellers?"

I just looked at him with a blank stare.

"You were wondering about the photographer who took the photo with the butterfly tattoo?" he asked. "It wasn't you. In that reality, there is a slightly inferior agent who received that task because you are enjoying a fruitful career as a writer. The Safe tried to recruit you but was unsuccessful."

I blinked. "Wait, are you suggesting that Sid is somehow responsible for my sister's death?"

"Put on your utilitarian hat for a minute, because I know you wear it well. You are an insanely good agent already, and you're still so young. Your potential has been on the agency's radar for a while. Sid knows what you are capable of and foresaw the scenario that would be successful in getting you to join the ranks. You could not thrive as a writer, and you also needed combating domestic terrorism to be a huge personal motivator. We don't know what other scenarios he attempted in order to successfully recruit you, and we cannot one hundred percent say that the bombing was causal and not just corollary. But the shoe certainly fits. And it still fits under the guise of international security."

I felt like I had been punched in the gut. All I could think of to ask in response was, "How do you know these things?"

"Let's just say I have hypnosis deeply embedded in my bag of tricks, and even Safe recruiters aren't immune to my abilities."

My heart was beating fast. The implications of what Alec had just told me were earth shattering. At best Sid was manipulating events on a criminal level—at worst, he had fully defiled free will.

My allegiance was shifting in real time. If what Alec said was true, and my gut knew that it was, Sid's power could not be left unchecked. And while I understood his reign had to be curtailed, it wasn't as simple as cutting off his power source. "Even if you were able to somehow take down Sid, which is a massive 'if', then what? The whole world, the whole multiverse, could erupt in chaos."

"That is what tyrants have threatened since the beginning of mankind. That without a governing body that mandates order, there would be dangerous levels of disorder. But the truth is that most people don't even know that Sid exists, so how could his absence be so readily exploited? It's scary to consider the unknown, but humanity functioned well enough before Sid's existence, and it will continue just fine after."

My head spun and I thought of the possibilities for my next course of action. I could team up with Alec on his suicide mission to bring down Sid. I could join the pro-privacy protesters. I could talk to the media about this and expose what had happened. I could confront the director head-on. I could literally run away to another universe and never look back. What I could not do was nothing.

But that was exactly what I'd have to do in order to effectively play Sid's game with any chance of winning. Absolutely nothing, for now.

CHAPTER 5

Neither of us spoke for what seemed like an eternity. Alec knew revealing my sister's fate was the trump card that would convince me to join him. He had effectively gained my trust, and now my support. We were unspoken allies in whatever war he was already waging. I thought about the other "me's"—who I could have been, my alternate destinies.

I was devastated over my sister, but also devastated by the future I'd never had a chance to pursue. Or at least pursue in this lifetime. It was confusing, both emotionally and mentally, to say the least.

Moments later a wave of extraordinary fatigue washed over me. I was emotionally drained and felt like I could sleep for twenty-four hours straight. I was so tempted to just curl up in a ball right there, on the edge of the world, and take a nap. I had forgotten we were on this theoretical physics-related border, and I felt so very far from home.

Alec must've sensed my exhaustion, because he held out his hand. I grasped it, and he began to walk me back through the tunnels as I followed in a stupor.

When we finally arrived back at the manhole we had entered through, I reflected on my otherworldly experience, quite literally. I had wrapped my mind enough around what had transpired to be able to collect myself and re-enter the world quite the same as I had left it—on the outside at least.

"When you hear a whistle, that's a signal I've set up to let us know when there is something obscuring the surveillance camera over this specific location. We have about a ten second window to emerge and continue walking to avoid suspicion," Alec said. "I'll give you a boost, but you'll need to get on your feet quickly. Start walking and continue on your day as usual, and we'll meet again soon."

"No," I replied, feeling emboldened. "We're not doing the cat and mouse thing anymore. We have too much to do and too much to discuss. Is there any reason why we can't meet up back at the park, and you can continue to flirt with me and we'll develop a not-so-platonic relationship?"

He looked a bit shocked, but by no means upset. "Really, Chase, are you asking me out right now?"

"Whether or not we'd be 'really' going out is a discussion for another time, but it seems like a pretty good cover. You've thoroughly laid the groundwork for it as far as I can tell."

"Well, if you're comfortable with that, I certainly am." He smirked. I felt a little lighter, and a much-needed smile crept onto my lips.

We emerged from the manhole at the right time, and in a tight embrace. The camera footage would show two young adults who had presumably sought out some alone time in an obscure alley. We walked back toward the park holding hands, both of us smiling, and it wasn't just an act.

It seemed as though a lifetime had passed since I left Hayley and the crew to go grab some water. In reality it had only been a little over an hour, an hour in which Hayley had finished a few Solo cups filled with white wine and hadn't really noticed my absence.

"There you are!" she exclaimed upon my approach. "I was just starting to get hungry and hoping you'd bring some snacks back with you." Her slightly misted eyes widened as she started processing that I was holding hands with someone, and whom that figure was.

"Look who I ran into! Alec remembered *us* from his performance at that club," I started. "We ran into each other just over there and we had a nice walk."

At first she looked skeptical, but her slightly intoxicated state ended up working in our favor. Alec just winked at her, and she beamed. "This is so wild! That must've been quite the walk considering this," she said, motioning to us holding hands.

"I'll fill you in later," I replied, also beaming.

At least that bought us a little bit of time to think our story through. "Should we all get some pizza?"

"I've never wanted anything more in my entire life," cried Hayley, always a fan of the dramatic. She pushed herself between Alec and me, put her arms around us, and led the charge to our favorite pizza joint.

Following Hayley's lead, we ate mostly in silence. Not because we didn't want to chat, but because we were entirely consumed by the pepperoni slices in front of us. Considering Alec and I needed to talk this through, the situation worked out well.

Afterward, Alec walked us back to our apartment and feigned being a gentleman. "Have a good rest of your day, you two," he said, starting to hug us goodbye.

"Absolutely not! You're coming inside with us—we have a lot to talk about!" Hayley grabbed us both and brought us upstairs to the living room. It was about thirty seconds before she declared she needed a nap and fell asleep on the couch.

Alec grabbed my hand and led me to my bedroom. "She was right," he said, "we do still have a lot to talk about."

"How did you know which room was mine?" He just rolled his eyes, and I remembered the feeling I'd had a few nights ago that someone had been watching. I didn't have the energy to care though; it seemed such a miniscule detail in the events that had played out since.

Seating in my room was sparse, so I motioned for Alec to sit next to me on the edge of the bed. He left a healthy two feet between us, so there was no mistaking his intent of having a "strictly business" conversation.

"So where do we start?" I asked. He looked at me with such intensity that I felt my cheeks turning red.

"Tell me about your day-to-day life at The Safe," he replied. Confidentiality had been so ingrained in my psyche that I was still reticent to open up.

"What do you already know?" I asked in response.

"Well, I know that you're an evidence collections agent and I'm vaguely familiar with what that entails in regards to using the loops for field work. But in order to help devise a plan that allows you to fly under the radar while collecting more intel about Sid's layers of protection, I need to know more about the people you work with."

I proceeded to tell him about my team members, including Brooke and my handler Caleb. Director Chambers came up next, and Alec seemed particularly interested.

"I mean I haven't worked personally with her," I said. "But she signs off on all missions. I see her talking with Caleb from time to time. She seems surprisingly accessible for such an authority figure."

It was well past bedtime when we finished talking through everything. I walked Alec out of my room. Hayley had at some point made it to her bedroom, so there was no need for an awkward goodbye.

He briefly kissed me goodnight and said, "I'll see you soon." Butterflies fluttered in my stomach as I watched him retreat. At the same time, I slowly started to process all that had happened. Returning to work tomorrow was not going to be easy.

"What has gotten into you?" Brooke asked me as I strolled in to work the next morning, seeming half amused, half suspicious. "I didn't think you had it in you!"

"I must admit, I surprised myself." I smiled big. "I was very much in need of some Vitamin D. Did I miss anything interesting?"

"Not really," she replied. "Same old. I heard Director Chambers wants a word with you though."

My stomach dropped. What had Sid pieced together?

My only response was "Oh?"

She sensed my concern, but mistook it for my do-gooder self fretting over being caught playing hooky, as opposed to the reality of my revelatory day with Alec being discovered. "I'm joking. We all passed around your photo here, and for the most part thought you deserved it, with the exception of Darren of course." She rolled her eyes dramatically.

I exhaled deeply, relieved.

The rest of the day was business as usual. It was hard to believe that everything had continued so normally while I was quite literally in another world. I reviewed the paperwork provided to me and saw that it was going to be a quiet day at my desk. There would be no field trips today.

That meant it was time to begin phase one of our plan.

CHAPTER 6

In order to promote an atmosphere of high achievement and self-improvement, The Safe had a quite a few programs to make their employees feel valued. One of these was "office hours" for those in leadership roles. Director Chambers was no exception.

Once a month, Chambers hosted a three-hour block in her office for anyone at The Safe to come and chat. Most employees, like Brooke, used this as an opportunity to suck up, pitch new ideas, and stay on the director's radar for promotion opportunities.

I had never taken advantage of this face-time with senior level staff, but I had good reason to now. I signed up for the next available office hours timeslot, the following Thursday at 2 pm. I needed to prepare accordingly. Subject line: Career Trajectory.

The main objective of meeting with Director Chambers was to learn as much about Sid's security as I could, but with the most subtlety I could muster. I was incredibly nervous about Chambers being able to see through my objectives, but Alec had reassured me that my charming demeanor would not lend itself to any suspicions of dubious motives.

Because Alec and I couldn't communicate openly via text or phone call, he swung by most days after work to check in. One evening, he picked up sushi and set up a rainbow display of raw fish along my kitchen counter. I had not yet acquired any semblance of appreciation for uncooked tuna, let alone the fleshy sea urchin that was now baiting me to lose my cool.

"Did you just witness a murder?" Alec asked, laughing at the look of horror that was so clearly plastered on my face.

"I don't do well with sushi," I sputtered.

"Well, we need to change that. When was the last time you had it?"

"A few years ago I tried a salmon and cream cheese roll and it did not go down well. It was just so, so, so slimy."

"Do you trust me?" he asked, and I nodded somewhat hesitantly. "Okay, close your eyes."

I obliged, and I felt him tip my chin up. I parted my lips and braced myself for the worst. Instead he kissed me softly, and my breath caught in my throat. My whole body tingled. "Are you ready for a sensational journey, Miss Silver?" he said in the most tantalizing voice.

With my eyes still shut, I mumbled, "Mmhmmm."

"I believe thoroughly in the power of positive association," he cooed. With that, he popped a piece of sashimi into my mouth. The fish was fresh and the sauce was tangy. It was nothing like what I remembered, or what I had dreaded. I smiled and pursed my lips at the same time.

"That wasn't so bad, was it?" I didn't want to give him such satisfaction, so I shrugged playfully. "Would you like another taste?" He kissed me again and popped another piece in my mouth. "Sushi is supposed to be consumed right away when it's freshest. Plus, it's taking up counterspace..."

I welcomed every bite.

I could still feel myself pulsing with adrenaline late into the night, but despite it taking hours to fall asleep, I woke up feeling refreshed. Most nights we had been able to focus and plan, but it was a welcomed break to simply enjoy each other's company.

The next day we were back to business as usual—and that wasn't a bad thing. Our relationship was stronger because of it. Maybe it was the product of not being able to obsessively analyze the true meanings of five-word text messages, which had become par for the course in the early stages of a modern relationship. But we were pretty much forced to be clear communicators from our "first day as a couple" since we were limited to in-person interactions. We both now shared a deep commitment to undermining Sid and agreed that the only way we would be able to do so was to prioritize the mission, and to be honest with ourselves and with one another. We stayed up many a night writing scripts for different scenarios that would allow me to gain access to the intelligence we needed. We essentially created tens of new aliases that I was fortunately already accustomed to adopting. I felt perpetually exhausted but empowered at the same time.

I suppose there's nothing quite like learning about infinite parallel universes that have defined your personal destiny to give you a renewed energy and perspective on life and relationships. So much of my world now seemed inconsequential. The only things that mattered were the people I cared about and, in essence, giving them their lives back. Removing Sid's control over their lives and restoring freedom—the potential to unleash free will—reduced most of my material priorities to dust.

Alec and I seemed to be very much on the same page, and he was so grateful to finally have a partner in all this. His confidence was contagious when I was with him. Unfortunately, it wavered a bit when I was on my own.

◆ ◆ ◆

I really could have used some of that confidence when I walked into Director Chambers' office that Thursday.

"Miss Silver, lovely to see you here. What brings you in today?"

She peered at me over her cat-eyed frames. Her hair was blonder than mine, pulled back in a tight knot. The tautness gave her a stern appearance, but she smiled with her eyes. I took the seat on the other side of her desk and marveled at some of the gadgets laid out in front of me.

"Hi Director, I wanted to take a few minutes of your time to discuss career opportunities here and the skills I need to acquire to be able to advance further." I smiled at her sweetly.

"I appreciate you taking the initiative, Chase. You'd be amazed at how many women here work fourteen hours a day for years without pursuing this conversation."

"Only women, ma'am?" I said, slightly caught off guard at her comment.

"Please don't take offense. I've just noticed during my time here that men are much quicker to ask for promotions. I believe that part of my responsibility as being a female leader is empowering other high-performing women leaders. But they need to make the initial ask."

Well, that was encouraging. Partly out of fear of making eye contact, I couldn't stop staring at this bizarre contraption on her desk that somewhat resembled a historical lava lamp from the 1960s, but with a lot more buttons around the base. When I looked closer, each neon blob that was slowly moving around was actually shaped like a continent.

"It's a lava globe," she said, following my gaze and tapping her well-manicured nails on the desk. "I love this piece, as odd as it is. One of our past analysts was actually somewhat of an artist. He made this based on how Sid views the world. The lava, or land masses, are not separate. If you look closely, they are all actually connected by the clear, 'invisible' liquid in between—and it's actually that liquid that dictates the lava's movement and interaction with every other mass."

"That's so cool," was all I could think to say.

She smiled and clasped her hands together in front of her. "Now, tell me what you like about your job now, and where you'd like to be next if you have an idea."

"I like being in the field; it's exciting. But I feel like I'm limited in what I can do because of the stove piping. I obviously understand the need for compartmentalizing information, but I think if I had a better understanding of the systems that we have in place to connect the information, it would help me become more of a leader. I'd love to be a decision-maker one day."

I was trying my hardest not to sound like I was reading off a script, and I hoped I was at least decently successful in my delivery. Alec and I had needed to reverse engineer the dialogue based on my true objectives. The "decision-maker" verbiage was an ad-hoc decision I was quite proud of, based on Director Chambers' prior comment about empowering female leadership.

"I see. Interesting," she replied. "As you know, we can't break down the barriers for communication for security reasons. But if you're interested in the 'how' as opposed to the 'why,' our information security unit is pretty high up in the ranks. This is by no means your average InfoSec unit and it is quite a prestigious place to land. Let me review some upcoming openings there and see if there's a fit. I can't promise anything overnight, but I'll see what I can do."

I thanked her profusely, and hoped she'd follow through in a timely manner. I could feel her eyes following me as I left the room.

I relayed the meeting to Alec that evening. "Well, that all sounds very promising," he said. "I think we've earned ourselves a break for a few days."

"What do you mean 'we'? All the pressure has been on me!" I exclaimed.

"Yes, but if it weren't for my impeccable

planning and strategy skills, where would you be right now?" I could hear the smile in his voice.

"I'd probably be content with my old ways, enjoying my work and simple social life." I meant to sound off-handed and coy, but to some degree it rang true. Would I have been better off right now if I had never gone to that club and met Alec? The point was probably moot, as Alec would have sought me out regardless. The thought of once again seemingly not having control over my own life put me in a somber mood.

As if reading my mind, Alec said, "You know, the work you are doing right now is benefitting the entire universe. It's a lot to swallow, but it would be tough to find a more purposeful life right now. That being said, I do think we both need a break. Is there anywhere you've been wanting to visit? I happen to know a few shortcuts..."

CHAPTER 7

As the clock struck five on Friday, I was already halfway out the door at work. Alec said he was taking me on a surprise weekend trip off the grid, and to meet him at the high-speed rail station halfway between The Safe and home. My train was already half empty when I boarded, and when I got off at the designated stop there was nobody around. I mean nobody.

There were rolling golden hills and I heard some cows mooing off in the distance. It was sunny and hot, but the eeriness of the deserted area left chills running down my spine. I sincerely hoped that we would be getting on another train, and soon.

My phone rang—Alec was calling me—and I immediately answered. "I really hope you're close by. This station gives me the creeps."

"Yeah, I'll be there in five. I'm in a gray avy." (That was slang for autonomous vehicle.)

Sure enough, he pulled up a few minutes later. He was sitting in the back and opened the door for me to hop in, barely stopping long enough to throw my bag in after me.

"You're right, this place is creepy. It just

worked out as being on the way to our turn off." The car veered south and we crept along a deserted road for about twenty miles.

Finally, Alec commented that we were almost there. I must have looked alarmed, because he laughed and patted me on the back—not reassuringly.

"Okay, I'm going to put a blindfold on you. And you have to do what I say," he said mysteriously.

"Um, I don't think so. I've really enjoyed being your girlfriend but I'm not really into that kind of thing." I laughed.

"No, really—put the blindfold on. I promise it will be worth it."

I did as he said.

I heard him slide open the door, but we were still moving in the car, not slowing down at all. He picked me up effortlessly like a toddler and slung me over his back, grabbed my bag with his free hand, and whispered in my ear, "Ready?"

Before I even had a chance to answer, he jumped out of the car. I shrieked, but we immediately landed on the softest sand I had ever felt in my life. I suspected we had fallen through yet another manhole. I heard waves crashing nearby and could smell the saltiness of the ocean. I somehow felt lighter and the air I inhaled was crisp and clean, but it was like breathing out of a seafoam-flavored oxygen tube. "Can I take my blindfold off now?" I practically begged.

"Once you've taken a few deep breaths, you can take it off." I figured he meant to enjoy the fresh air, but he really wanted me to relax.

When I removed the blindfold, at first I couldn't process what I was looking at. I had expected a yellow sand beach along the narrow delta, but this was unlike any destination I had seen in person before. Before me was an enormous calm body of water that had an almost lavender hue to it, and it stretched onward to the horizon. I looked up and the sky, too, was purple.

The sand below me was a pure, incredibly fine white, sticking to my feet when I raised and shook them. There was no other sign of life, but about fifty yards to my left I saw a small hut that appeared to be made of the sand I was standing in. It looked like a giant sandcastle modeled after a white brick, Gothic cathedral.

"Where the hell are we?"

"Welcome to my own personal paradise," began Alec. "I discovered this world by accident when I was first exploring the tunnels. There are tunnels all through the hills in that no man's land we just left. I've explored here quite a bit and there's nothing for miles. I've tested the air and water, and both are okay for ingestion. The salt you smell is actually from the sand. It's really more like a salt flat than a beach, and aren't the colors just breathtaking? I started bringing supplies here and set it up as a refuge in case my magic career ever turned south, but really I just like to vacation here." He motioned over to the castle. "I took Adderall one day and had a one-man sand-castle building competition, and now it makes for the perfect getaway." He winked.

"So let me get this straight. Instead of getting your own remote private island somewhere that would take hours to get to via hyperloop or days by commercial flying, you found your own tropical world right off the I-5 freeway?"

"Yes, isn't it lovely? And the best part is, the ozone here seems particularly strong—no climate issues in this world—so you don't even need to wear sunscreen."

I laughed as Alec unpacked food and games, and we just lounged around and relaxed for the rest of the day. It was indeed a much-needed escape.

On Saturday evening, Alec set out a blanket and picnic basket. We stretched out and snacked, and it was the most at-ease I had felt in a long time. When I had previously tried to ask about Alec's past, he always shifted uncomfortably and replied curtly. But I figured this might be the setting I needed to get him to open up to me.

"This is so perfect," I began. "I could just lie here forever."

He hugged me and smiled the most beautiful smile.

"Where do you see yourself after this whole thing is worked out?" I asked.

"You know, Chase, I'm not really sure. I actually do enjoy the intrigue and engagement that magic brings to my audiences. Maybe I'll keep doing that for a while. Though my disappearing act might get a bit more complicated. I have a feeling it won't be as easy to travel, if you know what I mean."

I smirked. "Is that what you always wanted to do when you were growing up?"

"More or less. I remember stopping in the park to watch a street mentalist when I was younger. I felt like he literally read my mind. Instead of asking myself how he did his tricks, I asked myself how I could learn to do them better. It seemed like the coolest skill in the world. I started researching mentalism here and there, and found out that I had a knack for it. I wasn't as good as the performers you pay money to see, but I saw an opportunity for some of the bigger stage acts that I thought I could re-engineer. It was just a hobby as a kid, but then once I was introduced to the tunnels—it quite literally opened up a lot of doors for me."

I nodded, and then broached another question that had been gnawing at me. "How did you find me, Alec?"

He looked as if he was weighing his words carefully. "I mentioned to you earlier that I'm quite adept at hypnosis. I made a point a while back of establishing a relationship with a recruiter at The Safe, and I learned about you from her. She also provided me with the information about the butterfly image, if you were wondering. She goes by the nickname 'L.'"

I hated myself for zeroing in on his use of the word "relationship," but I told myself he was here with me now, and a "let's talk about past relationships" conversation could definitely wait. Not wanting to spoil the evening, I simply nodded and curled up at his side.

That night I dreamed of the girl with the butterfly tattoo. We were in what seemed like a jungle, running as if something terrible were on our heels. I followed her into the depths of foliage that grew denser and denser. I kept calling out for her to stop and face me, but she kept running with her back to me. I tried to quicken my pace, but she was always just out of my grasp. My body shook with frustration as the bushes got so thick I could barely make it through, and darkness started to engulf me.

"Why won't you turn around and face me!?" I cried out, exasperated. When I was just about to give up, I made it through a particularly tangled bush and saw that the girl had stopped in a clearing. Light crept through the trees, and I entered what seemed like a circular grove.

Her back was still facing me, and my frustration suddenly transformed into fear.

I crouched down at the edge of the grove and she turned around slowly. This was the same girl from Singapore, but her eyes were hollow. It was as if someone else was looking through, trying to communicate with me.

"What do you seek, Chase?" she said, her voice chilled.

"I seek answers. I seek the truth," I replied.

"You're not ready. You are still trapped," she said. "Free yourself, and you will begin again."

Suddenly, I started crying and shaking uncontrollably, but I couldn't begin to comprehend why. I was in that state where I was aware that I was dreaming, but I was on the cusp of discovering something of immense importance, so I actively prevented myself from waking. But I couldn't get to the crux of it. All I could muster was, "Please, what is your name?"

"It's the name you wish you were born with," she said mysteriously. And with that, she vanished.

I woke up with a start, my heart racing. I was sure I must have cried out in my sleep, but Alec slept soundly beside me.

While this wasn't part of our well laid-out plan, I had to find out more about this girl. And I was pretty sure I knew where to start.

When I was growing up, I had a borderline unhealthy obsession with young adult novels. Maybe it was the writer in me craving for an escape, but I would pick up a book and physically be incapable of putting it down before I finished the whole thing. If my parents tried to make me go to sleep or come down for a meal, I'd throw a fit. I was the only student at school whose parents had to actively monitor a voracious school reading habit, instead of normal parents who pretty much had to force their kid to sit down and carve out time to read.

I was a very empathetic child, and I had a knack for bonding with the characters on the pages. My all-time favorite character's name was Lyra. She and I were the same age of eleven when I was reading *The Golden Compass* for the first time, and she felt like an extension of myself, with a much more interesting life. I wanted her life so badly that I made a "formal" request to my parents to have my name changed to hers. It didn't go over well, but that desire to carry her name remained a vivid memory from my youth.

Luckily, *Lyra* wasn't a very common name.

CHAPTER 8

My return home was uneventful. I wondered briefly if there were any physical implications of traveling between worlds, but then I reminded myself that I had been unknowingly doing so at my job for years with no obvious ramifications thus far. *Did I ever sign a waiver about hazards associated with inter-world travel?* I thought to myself. I bet that would be a big lawsuit one day, but then again Sid would never allow that kind of danger or exposure to The Safe's activities. But this did beg the question of who else knew about the inner-workings of what was going on at The Safe.

When I got into work on Monday, I was delighted to see a field assignment ready and waiting for me. It had been awhile since my last trip to Singapore, and I really did enjoy those assignments. Yet when I opened up my envelope, I immediately concluded there must have been some mistake.

The assignment letter on my desk was identical to my last. I'd never encountered anything like this before. It crossed my mind to check with my handler Caleb, but something told me to keep it to myself. Excitement fluttered in my stomach, as I realized I might get to see the girl with (or without?) the tattoo—whose name might be Lyra —in just a few short hours. I wished I could confide in Alec and discuss the implications, but there was no secure way of communicating with him while I was at work.

I left my desk to go collect my field items from my locker. I would wear the same disguise as last time. Once again resuming the identity of the high-end art consultant with a fabulous white jumpsuit, I made sure I had my camtact at the ready and made my way to the loops.

As I buckled myself into the capsule, I couldn't shake the feeling that something was off. And it wasn't just déjà vu from getting the same assignment. I couldn't abandon my post just because of a bad feeling, though, so I boarded the lift to my loop.

A few minutes later, I was back in Singapore. Literally everything was the same from the moment I stepped off the loop to the meeting at the coffee shop. It was like I had stepped back in time, a very unnerving feeling. I snapped the photos with my lipstick remote, and this time the girl did have a butterfly tattoo on her wrist.

My head spun as I tried to figure out if this was the same scene I had witnessed previously. Had I somehow traveled back in time through the loops? I sighed at my own inability to comprehend the universe around me, and made my way to the same food center where I had last gotten food poisoning.

As I headed toward lunch, someone bumped into me walking the other direction. She didn't stop to apologize. It was the lady with the tattoo —and she had slipped something into my bag. I almost called out "Lyra" after her but thought better of it. I was tempted to reach down and see what waited for me at the bottom of my purse right then and there, but reminded myself that Sid was always watching.

Just in case I had somehow traveled back in time, I decided to get a different dish that would not be at risk of contamination. This time I opted for pineapple fried rice, and the chicken was dry but thoroughly cooked. I made it back to The Safe without incident, and when I had a moment of privacy in the restroom later that afternoon, I seized it. I pulled out what Lyra had put into my bag—a crinkled piece of paper with some text scrawled across the middle. All it said was, *When the time comes to power down or power on, you'll find the key fits into your story.* A small rusted key fell into the palm of my hand, and upon examination, I found it quite unremarkable. I figured it would factor into our plan for Sid somehow, and I tucked it away in my bag. Something told me to keep the message to myself, though, so I didn't tell Alec.

Alec waved at me through the window as I walked up to my front door that evening. I followed him into the kitchen, relaying my day in vivid detail.

He sat there thinking to himself for a few minutes while I prepared dinner, keeping my racing mind at bay.

"It must have been a test," he said decidedly. "If you were trying to act like nothing had changed, like you hadn't learned anything new, you would have done everything possible to keep up appearances. That means you would have eaten the same food that made you sick the first time around. I think since you acted rationally and ate different food to avoid getting sick, it indicated that you weren't acting defensively. You passed."

"What? That makes no sense. What was I being tested on? Who was testing me?"

"I'd have to guess that Sid was just checking up on some of your anomalous behavior lately to make sure you haven't been 'compromised.'"

"What anomalous behavior?"

"Well, you did play hooky and take a sick day recently. That's not like you."

"Oh, I suppose you're right. So you think it's nothing to be worried about?"

"No, I don't think so," he said. But his eyes indicated otherwise.

The next morning, I saw I had a meeting on my calendar with Director Chambers. My stomach dropped, and for a fleeting second I thought about fleeing the country. What if she was on to me? But I had about zero chance of successfully escaping, and thus far I hadn't technically done anything against protocol, anyway. She probably had some other reason for wanting to see me—I hoped.

Collecting my wits, I headed to my meeting. I nervously waited outside of the director's office for a few minutes before the door slid open. "Agent Silver, please come in."

"Good morning, Director Chambers." My voice cracked, betraying my nerves.

"Sorry for bringing you in today without warning, but you're not in trouble. In fact, I have some exciting news for you," she said, sensing my trepidation. "We are promoting you to a senior officer role in the Information Security Department. You will now be reporting to the Head of Infosec, Dr. Kyle." She motioned to the stout man on her left, whom I had failed to notice until that moment.

"Thanks for the introduction, Director," said Dr. Kyle. "Agent Silver, it's very nice to meet you. Your record is most impressive, and I've heard wonderful things about you from both Director Chambers and your peers. It will be great to have you on our team."

Caught in the moment, I was very excited.

Getting promoted to that role at my age was indeed quite an accomplishment. "Wow, this is such an honor. I'm thrilled to be joining the team. Thank you!"

"You'll finish up your current projects this week and report to the Infosec Unit starting on Monday," said Chambers.

I nodded, smiled, shook their hands, and made a quick exit before they could ask me any questions.

CHAPTER 9

That weekend, Hayley and I went out for a little retail therapy. I was, after all, basically starting a new job—one of the few self-qualified events that demanded a wardrobe upgrade. The two of us walked into a boutique called Forever Young. Lined up against the left wall was a series of full-length mirrors with ladies marveling at themselves in tan leotards. It had been a while since I'd been shopping, and I'd forgotten about this part, maybe somewhat intentionally.

As we walked down the aisle, we each grabbed a leotard in our size and proceeded to the dressing room ahead. I put on the bodysuit and exited the room, stationing myself in front of an open mirror. My first thought as I looked myself over was that I looked tired. I noticed wrinkles under my eyes that I hadn't spotted before. I shuddered a bit in revulsion.

But before long, the mirror came to life in front of me. I was greeted by a cartoon-like lady on the side panel, asking if I was shopping for anything in particular.

"I'd like some new work outfits, as I'm starting a new role on Monday," I told the cartoon.

"Ah congratulations, Miss! That is exciting. Let me see what I can pull for you." She began virtually going through racks of clothes, pulling out pieces here or there and hanging them on the other side off the mirror panel. She brought over subdued dresses, skirts, blouses, shoes, and some other accessories. "Are you ready for outfit number one?" she asked. I nodded in response.

The cartoon snapped her fingers, and my tan leotard disappeared in the mirror, replaced by a lovely knee-length olive sweater dress, a loose beige vest, and tan ankle booties. She also took the liberty of replacing my ponytail with a vision of loose, wavy locks, and a fresh face full of makeup.

I loved it and told the cartoon to add it to my bag. This was going to be an expensive outing.

For the next forty-five minutes, Hayley and I took turns marveling at each other's image in the mirror. Since we were next to each other, we could glance over and provide commentary on the other's reflection. Of course, if we looked over directly, we'd just see each other in those awful leotards.

After greenlighting three more full outfits, two pairs of shoes, and a sparkly eyeshadow palette, I was ready to check out. I finalized my order with the cartoon. She automatically processed my transaction through my e-ID, and I was provided with three garment bags with my new belongings as I left the store.

Artificial intelligence these days had a lot of

benefits, but being so spot-on with my tastes and preferences was arguably not one of them, at least not for my bank account. But I tried not to dwell on the cost too much, and excitedly went home to try on the outfits again in the physical realm.

"You look beautiful, Chase," Alec commented as I came out dressed for dinner that evening in one of my new looks: high-waisted shorts and a loose V-neck blouse.

"Thanks." I blushed. "To be honest, I'm a little bit nervous about starting on Monday. I feel like I can't make any mistakes," I confessed.

"Quite the contrary," Alec said. "You want to build trust with your team, and know-it-alls and perfectionists are not known for being team-players. Just be yourself, focus on your day to day tasks, and you'll be fine."

I frowned at him.

Alec quickly backtracked. "I'm not saying *you* are a know-it-all or anything. Just that you don't need to worry about being perfect. Just be your kind, thoughtful self." Uh-huh.

On Monday morning, I headed to the Infosec Department. Brooke had left me a note in my locker wishing me the best, but I sensed underlying jealousy. I'd have to make lunch plans with her for later that week.

Dr. Kyle was waiting to introduce me to the team when I arrived.

"Good morning, team. I'd like to introduce you to our newest senior officer, Chase Silver," Kyle said. "Chase, why don't you tell the team a little about yourself."

"Thanks, Dr. Kyle, and hello everyone. It's wonderful to be here. I've worked as a field agent the last few years, I went to school down south, and I live in the city. Um, I'm sort of a homebody when I'm not hitting the loops for work." I smiled. "I'm really happy to be joining the team and am looking forward to working with all of you and getting up to speed."

Dr. Kyle nodded. "Thanks, Chase. I'm afraid most of your day today will be spent looking over your security clearance docs and signing all the paperwork." He transferred me an electronic document that spanned hundreds of pages.

"Let me know if you need anything," he added with an encouraging nod before I took a seat.

Two hours into the fine print, I came across an interesting passage:

> *When attempting to check for a breach, it is imperative that the conducting officer follows all relevant protocols listed in appendix 2a. If it appears that the hardware has been tampered with in any way, report this immediately to the most senior official who is on*

premises at the time.

The reason this piqued my curiosity was because I had never learned about hardware. His intelligence resided entirely within the cloud. What could possibly be held on a physical drive? There was no way a small piece of metal could be entrusted with the security or mechanical reliability necessary to house Sid's intelligence. Maybe stealing this "hardware" would be an easy solution to breaking Sid. I couldn't wait to get home and share this news with Alec.

"Penny for your thoughts?" A deep voice awakened me from my daydream.

I looked up and saw a young man who looked quite familiar. He was pale, with clear eyes and light hair. He looked only slightly older than myself, and I had not encountered many peers in my age group during my tenure at The Safe. "Oh, hi. Yes, I suppose my eyes started to glaze over. I'm not used to so much legal jargon. I'm Chase, by the way."

"I'm Taylor," he said. "And I was very excited to hear you worked here, let alone that you were joining our unit."

"Have we met before?" I asked, puzzled.

"No, not really. But I'm actually quite a fan of your boyfriend. Sorry, that must sound weird," he mused. "I'm a bit of a hobbyist magician myself, so I've been following Alec for a while now. I happened to see you two walking together a few weeks back in the city. Sorry, that probably makes me seem creepy and stalkerish."

"A bit," I said, taken aback. Alec and I were definitely not trying to be seen in public together, but I suppose we had gotten a bit lax in recent weeks. "I'd be happy to introduce you sometime," was all I could think of to say.

He beamed. "That would be awesome. Does he practice any tricks on you?"

"I could tell you, but then I'd have to kill you," I jested. "What type of magic are you into?"

"Illusions mostly. I've always been intrigued by the power of observation. That's how I landed up here, I suppose." His eye twitched and he looked uncomfortable, as if he momentarily regretted his last statement.

"What do you mean?"

"Well, you'll learn soon enough, but so much of what we do in the Infosec Unit is about finding anomalies that are invisible to most people. Good magicians exploit the fact that the majority of the population is exceedingly unobservant. There is immense power in being able to see the unseen." His last few words came out with an intentionally dramatic flair.

I laughed freely and made a mental note to dig a little deeper during our next conversation. He could be a great source for intel, and having one potential ally wasn't bad for a first day.

The rest of the day flew by surprisingly fast, as I had a ton of onboarding to catch up on. The contrast between the transparency of this team compared with the stealthy structure of my last was quite shocking. The Infosec team almost ironically seemed overly collaborative. They discussed the problems they encountered and seemed to brainstorm solutions together.

The rationale for this contrast was that they were working on the same potential threats— predicting and protecting The Safe from breaches together. This was different from having individual operative assignments that needed to be highly compartmentalized to maintain such a high standard of security. From a day to day perspective, I saw this as a huge upgrade.

For my longer-term plan with Alec, it was quite the opposite. When I relayed the new team dynamic, he was not amused, especially when I mentioned the exchange with Taylor.

"Are you jealous?" I half-joked.

"This isn't funny. We're supposed to be flying under the radar. And now one of your colleagues in the Information Security Department at The Safe knows we are together and is interested in our relationship." Alec sighed, looking genuinely concerned.

"What if he'll help us?" I asked.

"That's such a huge risk, Chase. I think that's a pretty ridiculous idea considering you just met the guy." I must have looked hurt, because he quickly added jokingly, "And, well, he clearly doesn't have great judgement or taste considering his deference to a certain magician." He winked and rested his hand on the small of my back.

Still unable to resist his charm, I laid my head on his shoulder.

"I know, I know," I murmured into his ear. "And I'll try to be more careful in the future. But he already knows about us, so there's nothing we can do about that now. We just need to figure out where to go from here."

"What do you propose?"

I turned my head to meet his gaze and ran my fingers through his hair. "He could be a good source of information. Why don't I just continue to be amicable with the guy and see where it leads us? I promise I'll tread carefully."

Alec nodded thoughtfully, so I took that as a blessing and ran with it.

The next day at work, I asked Taylor if he'd help me get up to speed a bit quicker. "I'm just plowing through the onboarding materials and I'm so excited to get started," I told him. "I'm a quick study, but I always learn better when it's a more dynamic, interactive environment."

"I'd be happy to help. Just let me know any questions you have and if you want to set aside a designated time to discuss," my new friend replied with a smile.

"Thank you so much, Taylor. Maybe we

could do a working lunch this week?" He was up for it, so we made plans accordingly.

As we walked to lunch together, Taylor asked, "How are you liking it so far working with the team?"

"It's honestly been a bit of a surprise—the day to day anyway. Everyone is really welcoming and kind. But it seems like there's not as much to do as I was expecting. That probably sounds naïve, so please jump in and correct me. Everything I'm reading indicates that Sid does most of the heavy lifting when it comes to his own security, though. I'm not entirely sure how we fit in."

We started piling food on our plates. I opted for a hearty salad with a scoop of cranberry chicken salad. Taylor got the same.

"I can see why it would feel that way," he said. "Obviously, Sid is the best resource for finding potential security threats, since he can see them coming a mile away from the outside. But if he did miss something, we still need to secure him from the inside if that makes sense. Sure, he's not vulnerable to malware or that sort of thing. But there are very sophisticated hackers out there who try to breach his walls on a daily, if not hourly, basis. They can get pretty creative."

"Have any gotten in?" I asked.

"How much of a data science background do you have?"

I shrugged. "I have a bit of a scattered background. Degrees in computer science with a concentration in data science, and creative writing. Hopefully those skills suit my role as more of a creative program management officer on this team, but admittedly my coding could be better."

"Okay, then I'll spare you the technical jargon. We haven't had any major breaches, thankfully, but there have been some inconsistencies that we have been investigating lately. We're not sure where they are coming from or if they are at all significant. Essentially, the confidence threshold in certain areas has been lowered, meaning Sid is less confident about the recommendations that he is providing."

As we made our way to a table and sat down, Taylor continued, "So it's not an overt breach or anything like that. There is just something we're keeping an eye out for that is prohibiting Sid from doing his job as effectively as usual. He's collecting the same amount of data, but something or someone is making him lower his confidence in his predictions based on that data. This doesn't mean his predictions are in any way flawed, but normally his confidence is over 99.9 percent, and we've had to lower it to 99.7 to continue to operate as usual."

I must have looked confused.

"So, that means in order to keep our operations going, we have to proceed with only 99.7 percent confidence that Sid's predictions are accurate instead of 99.9 percent. I know that seems like a small difference..."

"No, I understand the implications. Who made the decision to lower the threshold though?" I asked, frowning. One-fifth of a percent less accuracy when dealing with such a massive scale was quite shocking. I couldn't believe Taylor was being so cavalier, discussing this openly with me over lunch. This meant that Sid could potentially be wrong about 1 in every 500 recommendations, which could affect tangential recommendations, and continue to result in more flaws.

Taylor gave me an odd look. "Well, Sid dictates the confidence threshold of course! We're just working with that information and trying to find the cause of this discrepancy."

"Have there been any solid theories so far?" I asked.

Glancing down, he shook his head and moved the chicken salad around his plate a bit before digging in.

CHAPTER 10

When we returned to our desks, Dr. Kyle asked to have a word with me. It didn't seem like I was in trouble, but I still couldn't help my throat constricting as I followed him to his office.

"How are your first few days going, Chase?" he asked, shutting the office door behind us.

"Quite well, sir. I think I'm getting up to speed quickly. Taylor has been very kind in taking me under his wing."

Dr. Kyle sat down behind his desk, picking absentmindedly at the dirt under his nails. He motioned for me to take a seat, and glanced behind me at the door as if he was expecting someone to open it again. After a moment, he continued, "Well, I'm glad to hear that. He's a great asset for the team. I think you'll both be working fairly closely over the next few weeks too."

"Oh, that's great. He has been explaining the inner workings of Sid's confidence levels to me." I hated that I could be a nervous talker at times.

He refocused his gaze from the door back to me, and I could tell he was considering if I was intentionally trying to pry. "Yes, that certainly keeps our team busy. Would you like to come take a look this afternoon?"

"A look at...?"

"Sid's throne room, of course."

I tried to keep my cool, but I hadn't previously understood that my new assignment would allow me front row access to Sid so quickly, considering I hadn't even known about this "throne room." This was too good to be true, being offered the opportunity to examine Sid up close in the vast room that contained his hardware. Sure, Sid primarily resided in the cloud, relying on his cloud-based network that weaved in and out of the multiverse. But there was something so alluring about seeing him in 3D—well, as physically tangible as he could get. This could be huge for our plan.

"Excuse me, I need to check on something," he said. "But I'll come grab you a bit later." He showed me to the door and quickly shut it behind me.

I returned to my desk, signaling all was well to Taylor with a quick thumb's up. Similar to my unfortunate cases of periodic word vomit, I also reflexively used cheesy gestures from time to time.

Later that afternoon, Dr. Kyle guided me through a labyrinth at The Safe that had altogether been unknown to me previously. He continued to watch me with curiosity, as we ventured through the maze of halls and nondescript, unmarked doors. We seemed to be miles away from the loops, and it crossed my mind multiple times that if Dr. Kyle asked me to wait and he left, I'd probably die of starvation trying to find my way out.

"Apologies for having to cut you off so abruptly earlier, Miss Silver. Director Chambers needed a quick word, and it's never good to keep the director waiting," he said as we walked alongside one another.

"No apologies necessary. I know that your schedule is packed and I'm just grateful you're taking the time to show me Sid...that is still where we are going, right?"

He laughed. "Yes of course, it's just a bit of a trek. And it's a good excuse for me to get some steps in today."

After what seemed like two hours of walking in concentric circles, we stopped suddenly. Dr. Kyle stood in between two doors, and tools that were invisible to me apparently took his vitals, scanned his retinas—and all ten fingers.

Then the wall in front of me vanished.

"Sir?"

"Yes, it's quite amazing, isn't it? You just don't know what is physically real in here until you're asked to walk through it."

I could see he was testing me to see if I'd encountered anything like this before.

"But how does a wall just disappear, sir?"

"You know the technology here is simply astonishing," he answered vaguely. "I don't quite understand how it works myself. But if you'll follow me through, we can take a look at all the wonder that is Sid in the real world."

Hesitantly, I walked in after him. It was pitch black at first, and as we stepped through, the floor progressively lit up our path. I tried to take mental notes, but it was downright impossible to judge the size or any details at first as our eyes adjusted. The shapes seemed to solidify only as we came within arm's reach of them.

The floor lights had an orange glow that contrasted with the blue light emitted from the walls. As my eyes continued to adjust, I realized the walls surrounding us were comprised of an enormous screen, with billions of zeros and ones spanning the length of at least a dozen football fields.

"What the hell?" I gasped. I couldn't stop myself.

"It's somewhat of a shock, I know," said Dr. Kyle. "It feels like you are actually inside Sid's world, doesn't it? Now if you look above and below the screen, you'll notice towers extending in both directions. Those are the *drives*, for lack of a better descriptor."

I pulled my eyes away from the enormous screen that seemed to extend to the horizon, and indeed there were cascading black towers that looked like the skyscrapers and those floor scrapers in Singapore. It was a sight to behold. As I was taking it all in, I was still very conscious of Dr. Kyle watching my every move.

"Dr. Kyle," I decided to ask and confront the awkwardness, "are you worried I'm going to break something?"

"What? No, of course not. It's just a lot to take in, so I like to make sure that the newbies are carefully guided through this...experience," he said uncomfortably.

"Oh, ok. It is a lot to take in, that's for sure. What else should I see or know about while we're here?"

"Well, you've looked through the initial paperwork and should be fairly familiar with how this all works—on a non-technical level of course. What questions do you have for me?"

I had one big one but was unsure whether this was the time and place for it. *No time like the present,* I told myself.

"There are the rumors about the key, of course." I couldn't help myself. "Is it true there's a master switch somewhere in here?"

"Ah yes, everyone always asks about that. There is a 'master key' if you will, but it's not what you'd think of in the traditional sense. It's not a simple piece of metal that fits into a lock. Even if you were to get a hold of it, there's no way to turn it off. Well, no way for *you* to turn it off. The energy that powers it is a force to be reckoned with; it's bound together at a quantum level. You'd have to mess with the most sophisticated of quantum mechanics in order to power it off. So, there's not really any harm in showing you. It is a privilege that only a handful of people have, though, so don't take it for granted."

He could have easily been messing with me, as I didn't understand much of what he'd just said, but I did catch the part where he said he would take me to it. I told him as much, and he laughed, which lightened the mood significantly.

I followed him for another five minutes, trying to take mental notes of our path. Soon I saw before me a golden sphere that appeared to be floating in mid-air. I squinted and saw little sparks flying all around it.

"There it is," Dr. Kyle said. "It lives within that golden orb; you can think of it like a nucleus —protected by billions of atoms that are bound together. You'd need the equivalent of a hydrogen bomb to shut that thing off, and maybe even then it wouldn't work."

That was disheartening. I didn't have too many hydrogen bombs lying around. I couldn't deny, though, it was incredibly impressive and arguably beautiful. I took in as much detail as I could, hoping Dr. Kyle just saw me as an incredibly mesmerized employee. It wasn't untrue.

I suddenly had a million questions, and I began rattling them off. Dr. Kyle patiently answered them. I think that's what he was looking for, to make sure I bought in to the amazing technology that was Sid.

While I was still unsure whether his interest in my reactions toward Sid was routine or prompted by an external force, I felt more confident that I'd appeased him—more so than I had this morning anyway.

Yet seeing Sid and his impressive golden orb of protection up close put that recently acquired confidence in check.

Alec had never been so focused as he was in the days following that excursion. He was one hundred percent heads down, researching as much as he could about the possible mechanics of the throne room and Sid's "container." I continued along my normal routine at work, which was admittedly refreshing.

Taylor and I were hitting it off, platonically of course, and I soon considered him one of my closer acquaintances. It was nice taking the back seat for a bit on this crazy route my life had taken, and it seemed like I could just work hard and enjoy my days without consequence for a bit. But it had been two weeks since my tour of the throne room, and we had no leads. I wasn't overly stressed about it, but Alec was. I thought we could use an escape.

As Alec accompanied me back from the corner market one evening, I asked if we could return to his secret beach for the weekend. He merely shrugged as though he was only half paying attention to my request. There was something he couldn't work out, and it was consuming him.

"I'm here for you, Alec. Can we talk about whatever is puzzling you?"

"We can discuss it, but it will be moot. Chase, I'm sorry I haven't been as attentive lately. But, all the research and my admittedly primitive calculations are not looking good. I know there has to be a way though."

"Okay, well we've laid out all the groundwork. You have someone with access to the most secure room on the planet, possibly the universe, available to do your bidding," I replied, trying to lighten the mood.

"Don't you think I know that? It's killing me that we're so close and I can't figure out this last hurdle." He finished walking me back but hesitated for a moment at the front door. "I need some space to think through things. We'll talk later," he said, turning around to leave. I stared at his retreating back blankly.

Checking in on "my feelings" wasn't something that I often did, but in that moment, I realized that I wasn't mad he'd left, or really even sad for that matter. I just shared his frustration about our lack of recent progress and wanted to do something about it.

There was just no way to harness the kind of energy we needed to break Sid, and even if some kind of vessel existed, we'd then have to figure out a way to sneak it in,

Alec may not have wanted to escape for the weekend, but I realized that rest might be exactly what I needed. My best ideas often came during the night when I was sound asleep. My subconscious mind was a powerful one, and I begged for it to work with my conscious self to arrive at a solution. With that in mind, I gave myself permission to take a lot of naps on the weekends and go to sleep really early during the week.

One crisp Friday night in the city, I was reading in bed with a glass of deep red wine by my bedside. I grabbed another blanket to fight the chill and reached perhaps an unprecedented level of comfort. As I often did while reading in bed, I started to drift off and did not try to fight the urge to sleep.

I saw Lyra in my dreams that night, and I knew she would help me find some answers.

We were in the throne room, which looked very similar to when I had visited a few weeks prior, except there was a misty haze that obscured the floor so it felt like we were floating. The ethereal effect was quite nice. Lyra started to glide through the labyrinth that made up the room, and I followed. The room started to transform; a thousand mirrors sprang up around us. It was like a funhouse, where you looked into one mirror only to see an infinite number of reflections. When we were surrounded by mirrors, Lyra looked up and I followed her gaze. The gold orb was floating just out of arm's reach.

"Do you have the key?" she asked me. The key materialized in my hand. Although it wasn't the same key I was familiar with, this one had a very sharp edge. "Look in front of you," she instructed me next. I did, and I saw an infinite number of reflections staring back at me.

I looked at myself in the mirror, and in the corner of my left eye appeared a hole with a jagged edge. I slipped the key in and turned it sharply, forcing the glass mirror to break and the infinite number of reflections to shatter with it. I yelled out in confusion, but Lyra had gone. I woke with a start.

Feeling a bit winded, I wandered into the bathroom to splash some water on my face. As I looked up at the mirror, the realization of what my subconscious had just uncovered began to sink in. My heart rate quickened and beat strongly in my chest, but this borderline anxiety quickly transformed into emotional exhaustion, which soon translated into physical exhaustion.

Glancing at the clock, I groaned at the 3:18 time stamp. I crawled back into bed, took a few deep breaths, and somehow convinced myself to go back to sleep.

The aroma of bacon and eggs awoke me the next morning. I stumbled out of the room in a groggy stupor and was quite shocked to see Alec in the kitchen scrambling away.

"Breakfast?" he asked with a smile that made me realize how I missed his old cheery self.

"Yes please, what's the occasion?" I asked.

"You, of course!"

Ah, it was my birthday. I had completely forgotten given everything else that was going on. I had just departed my mid-twenties, but really it felt like I was entering a new decade.

"Thanks, Alec. It's just going to be another day at work though." I sighed. I did love birthdays, and they only came once a year. I was quite mad at myself for letting it slip my mind.

"Well, let's do dinner tonight. I have a little something planned." He pecked me on the cheek as I spooned scrambled eggs in my mouth. As a I glanced down, I was reminded of the cheesy stunt he pulled when we first met. He had bent a spoon "at will"—and told me that I could do anything if I put my mind to it. I smiled at the reverie.

The hours ticked by, and my vivid dream from the night prior became muted in the background of my mind. My team had a beautiful cake prepared after lunch, and I welcomed the slight uptick in attention. I did love a good yellow cake and chocolate frosting combo, and I enjoyed my piece immensely, all my worries forgotten for the time being.

What can I say, it's a wonderful thing to have your birth recognized. Dr. Kyle gave me a sturdy handshake, and Taylor awkwardly tried to get the team to sing a quick round of "happy birthday." I definitely appreciated the attempt though.

CHAPTER 11

Alec had told me to dress up, and I gladly obliged. It was nice to have him back in a cheery mood, so I didn't ask too many questions. I rummaged through my closet and found a silky lavender number with three-quarter sleeves and a tight bodice that called out to me.

We sat down at this hip Italian spot, and Alec ordered a nice bottle of Pinot Noir. As we ate our way through the salad and first course of homemade pasta, the wine began to dull my senses a bit. I was laughing and made a comment about wanting more nights like this and less that were bogged down in "mission-" related work.

"Sometimes I just go back and question why we're doing all this. At face value, our lives are wonderful. We get to enjoy life's luxuries, have each other and fulfilling work. It's the dream," I said nonchalantly.

He looked alarmed. "Chase, you're joking, right?"

"Well, I'm half joking. Obviously, I'm committed to what we're doing but it's also nice to reflect on how much we have."

Something about that last statement set

him off. "None of it is real if Sid is behind the wheel. You can't forget that."

I suppose we had traveled too far down this path for this to be in any way a joking matter, so I took a deep breath and made a conscious choice to focus on my food. I'd spoiled the mood, so without much additional conversation we finished dinner and went back to the apartment. But I couldn't get his comment out of my mind, and it festered.

By the time we got back, I was over-whelmed with emotion. I headed straight for my bedroom, shutting the door quickly behind me. As I collapsed on my bed, the tears started to stream down my face. I realized that I wasn't actually mad at Alec, but rather his statement reminding me that nothing was real.

All of my wants and needs were accounted for. I reminded myself that I had an incredibly impressive career (and work ethic to go along with it), I had reliable and dependable friends, and I should have been very happy and content with my life. But I wasn't. I acknowledged that it was natural to be overly dramatic and reflective on one's birthday, but I couldn't stop. My thoughts were spiraling.

Everything I did had been predetermined. I was not in control; I was just one of many possibilities that Sid had already observed and influenced. How was a person supposed to feel genuine joy or accomplishment under that kind of premise? The memories of my sister and scraps of paper that could have become works of written art began flooding my consciousness.

It was then that the implications of my dream from last night came roaring back. As much as I welcomed sleep, it never came. Adrenaline had taken its place. A plan was taking shape, and it was better if Alec didn't know about it.

◆ ◆ ◆

There was no hurry in my step the next morning as I considered my course of action. I walked at a leisurely pace throughout the labyrinth of The Safe until I found my desk. Despite my lack of sleep, I felt both energized and motivated to see it through.

"How were the birthday festivities?" Taylor asked, walking over to my desk.

"Dinner was delicious. You'll have to try the spot sometime. The homemade pasta was close to the best tasting dish I've had."

"That's quite the review!"

"Yep. Listen, Dr. Kyle took me to see Sid the other day and I've had some questions about its infrastructure that I just haven't been able to get past. Is it a big deal to go take another look?"

"We need to get it approved, but that's one of the perks of being on this team. You just need to have a good reason."

"Okay, how do we get the approval?" Taylor motioned toward Dr. Kyle's office. "Got it." I smiled.

"I can come with you if you'd like."

My first inclination was to protest, but I couldn't think of a logical reason to explain why he shouldn't accompany me. I nodded, my insides squirming.

"Taylor, you know how you were explaining to me about the inconsistencies in the confidence threshold in recent weeks? What if it's related to some sort of mechanical issues? Like there's something wrong with the hardware that is making Sid less confident about his analysis?"

Taylor looked at me, puzzled. I wasn't sure if it was because he was thinking through my proposal or if he was just confused by my feigned ignorance on the subject matter. I knew my suggestion was definitely a stretch.

He walked into a small soundproof office and motioned for me to follow. "Chase, here's the thing. We're not sure what's causing the inconsistencies, but it has something to do with you."

"*Me?*" The alarm must have been plastered across my face because he quickly moved to comfort me.

"You didn't do anything wrong, not yet, anyway. Sid's report just indicated that there is some sort of anomaly associated with you, but didn't let on to much else. But now I'm wondering if it has something to do with what you just proposed, and you tampering with the key—accidentally of course."

I took a second to process what he'd just said. Maybe this was why Dr. Kyle had been so cautious and ponderous when he took me to visit Sid. Maybe this was why my promotion had gone through so easily to begin with. It was all part of investigating this anomaly. I guessed it had to do with my unauthorized trips through the tunnels and traversing the multiverse covertly.

But, did Taylor and Dr. Kyle know about the multiverse and Sid's true standard operating procedure? If so, what did they know about me? What was safe for me to relay at this point, considering I was only supposed to see Sid as an incredibly advanced AI?

I decided to poke a bit.

"Taylor, that's ridiculous. Why would Sid adjust based on an alleged tampering that hasn't occurred yet?"

"We're not the only ones acting on his predictions; he's acting on them too," he said simply. "I am curious to know what you would do that would cause this issue though. I think we should go and talk it through without you actually touching anything. That should be harmless."

"All right. I'm not sure I fully understand, but if that makes sense to you..."

"I'll go speak with Dr. Kyle and see what he says." With that, he left the room and went over to Dr. Kyle's office. I could vaguely make out their outlines through the glass divider and it seemed like they were talking for a while. At the very least, it didn't seem like Taylor's ask was being outright rejected, so that was a positive.

Shortly after, Taylor reentered the room accompanied by Dr. Kyle. Dr. Kyle came over to my desk, casually resting his hand on the corner. "Chase, Taylor explained his reasoning and I think it makes sense to take another visit to the throne room. How's tomorrow afternoon? I have a few meetings today and I'd like to be there to observe."

I glanced up at him, trying to discern any glimmer of suspicion. He seemed to be his cool and collected self. "That would be great, sir. I'm looking forward to learning more," I said vaguely. I rubbed my palms together to disperse the sweat that had collected.

The conversation was brief, surprisingly natural, and left me feeling like I had dodged a bullet.

Sleep would not come again that night, but I was not tired. I lay in bed for hours, thoughts churning over and over in my head. When I had completely given up on sleep, I decided to get some fresh air. I walked around my neighborhood, taking in the pre-dawn sights. It was therapeutic, walking with nowhere to go, with no destination in mind. As I

considered my imminent actions and their ramifications, I toyed with the idea of finding Alec and
filling him in. But it was simpler this way. I didn't
want to give him the opportunity to try to stop
me.

I was having an out of body experience, and
my thoughts seemed to both blur and solidify at
the same time. My body continued to step forward but was merely acting out of habit.

Somehow I found myself at one of my favorite points in the city. High up on a hill, the
city lights flickered around me in the distance.
As I looked out at the water surrounding the city
and beyond, there was such stillness—almost like
the world was waiting for me to make my next
move. I felt calm for the first time in weeks; well,
my body felt relaxed with the exception of my
pounding heart.

When I returned home and got dressed for
work, I spent a little extra time tidying up my
place. Maybe I was procrastinating, but dusting
off the windowsills and giving the sink an extra
rinse seemed necessary. I even ironed my pants for
the first time in what seemed like years. Actually,
that might have been the first time I ironed my
pants ever. As I returned my freshly pressed pants
to their drawer, a glimmer caught my eye. I pulled
out the trick spoon from when Alec and I first met
and placed it delicately on my bed for him to find.

I locked the deadbolt as I left, not sure of the
next time I'd be able to return home. My commute

was uneventful, as was the morning spent at my desk. I dedicated a lot of my time to staring at the clock, waiting for Dr. Kyle to grab Taylor and me. Finally, at 2:43 pm, he came over and asked if we could go now as he didn't have another meeting scheduled until 4 pm. I nodded, and Taylor walked over to join us.

"Let's go, you two," he said. Taylor and I fell into step behind him.

The three of us began the zigzagging journey to the throne room. Taylor and Dr. Kyle were jabbering on about a budgetary issue that I was admittedly paying very little attention to. I was rethinking my logic and plan for what seemed like the thousandth time and felt as unsure as ever. But I knew I was as ready as I was ever going to be.

We got to the room and slowly started closing in on the gold orb. The extensive screen display seemed to engulf us, as I could still not get over the sheer massiveness of this room, if you could even call it that. It was more like a cavern. I was looking for a small stretch of darkness, an area not illuminated by numbers on a screen. A wall of nothingness proved to be incredibly challenging to find though.

I continued to circle Sid's epicenter, looking all around for nothing. Yet I soon realized that my naked eyes were not up to the challenge. When Alec and I had visited the tunnels at our initial park meetup what seemed like a lifetime ago, the nothingness had looked like a wall to me. I had to change my perspective.

"Is there any way to alter the display on these screens?" I asked, nodding toward the remote controller in Dr. Kyle's hand.

"It's one screen, Chase," Taylor said. Seeing my confusion, he added, "So it takes an incredible amount of energy to alter it, but we can do simple things like adjusting the contrast or brightness like you would on a PC."

"Okay, can we do that and change the contrast to make it as dim as possible?"

"Yes, I suppose so, but why?"

"I just have a theory." I smiled, hoping it looked innocent.

"Chase, this is highly irregular and I'm not sure I understand your rationale," said Dr. Kyle. "I think it's best we start heading back. You got your second look."

"Dr. Kyle, how do you know about this anomaly? I assumed it just came across in one of Sid's reports, but I never did ask," I said, trying to stall.

Dr. Kyle stopped quickly, Taylor at his side. "What anomaly are you referring to exactly?"

"The fact that I have something to do with the lower confi—" I looked at Taylor and then back to Dr. Kyle.

There was a brief pause. Dr. Kyle looked bewildered, and Taylor looked like he was quickly calculating. And so was I.

At that moment, so much clicked into

place. I realized that Taylor had fed me all the information about the anomaly and I hadn't actually spoken to Dr. Kyle about it directly. Taylor also knew about Alec, and had tried to get close to me from day one.

Before I could finish my train of thought, Taylor clocked Dr. Kyle hard under the left side of his chin. Dr. Kyle fell to the floor, and I just stared at Taylor quizzically.

"He's just knocked out," he said nonchalantly. "Thanks for helping me see what I was missing, Chase. You're now going to help me get to the other side."

"But why? Why didn't you just use the loops?" I guessed he was after access to the multiverse, but I was also trying to distract him. There was a mole after all, and he had led me here under false pretenses.

"Being able to traverse parallel worlds? That's ultimate power. But only when it's yours to control, and you know as well as I do that the loops don't offer any room for autonomy or deviation. I knew when you transferred into our unit that Alec had gotten to you and that you were working on access to the other worlds. Like I said, I've been following him for a while."

"No one should have that much power," I replied, thinking about Alec's unprecedented access to the multiverse and how that could be abused in the wrong hands. This is exactly what I had been working to prevent. I realized then that he had just fed me the entire story about the anomaly and compromised confidence levels to create a dependency between us. I didn't know if he understood what I was about to do next, but I had to move quickly to now thwart Taylor in addition to being able to see my plan through.

"What did you tell Kyle then?" I asked.

He shrugged. "I just fed him a story about it being a surprise birthday present from the team to allow you a second look. It is quite a sight to behold."

At that moment, we both dove for the small remote controller Dr. Kyle had been holding, but Taylor got to it first. Soon the white ones and zeros dipped to a dark gray, and the darkness engulfed us.

I did a quick visual scan, and then I saw it. I couldn't judge how far away it was, but I saw a barely perceptible line hovering in the distance. It didn't even look three dimensional. I started walking quickly toward it, but it didn't seem to get any closer.

Taylor yelled after me, "Where are you going?!"

Before long I broke out into a full run, Taylor at my heels. It never got any larger though, and I slowed to a jog. Even though the line didn't get bigger, as I moved side to side, I saw a shimmer. I ducked behind one of the towering beams, hoping Taylor would lose sight of me just for a moment.

"Chase, just hold on a second. We're on the

same team here."

I didn't say anything, but I was pretty sure he didn't understand my end game, and that was a huge advantage.

Keeping my body still, I started turning my head slowly back and forth. Finally, I reached an angle where my vision lined up so that the line looked almost like the edge of a sheet of glass. It was subtle, but I could see a bit of a reflection around the edges.

I saw an almost imperceptible shimmer of gold in that reflection, and in that instant, I knew I had been right.

As I started to shift my head again, Taylor grabbed me from behind and put me in a choke-hold. I gasped for air but didn't struggle. He was irrefutably stronger than myself, and I wasn't going to win with brute strength.

"Show me how to walk through to another universe, Chase. Then I'll let you go and we can be on our separate ways. I have a whole plan for myself on the other side."

"You have absolutely no idea what you'll be walking into, but if you get trapped in another world, what do I care?" He choked me tighter. "We need to walk toward that line over there," I said, gasping for breath.

"Why?" He wasn't easing up.

"There's a doorway here where the lining between worlds is thin. It's just over there, but it's easy to miss." I was only half lying.

"Okay, go slowly," he said, keeping hold of my neck and carefully following my every step. I wasn't going to break free.

Instead, before I could talk myself out of it, I slowly removed the small key that had been impressively weighing down my bag since Singapore. With the key in hand, I reached out toward the line. I extended my arm so that only the tip of the key looked as if it could reach the edge, if you looked at it just right. But that was enough.

"Easy, Chase, what are you—" His eyes widened in fear.

An intensely sharp and powerful energy emanated from the key to my fingertips. It was like a tidal wave that built up quickly, ready to explode. I was tied to the spot, completely immobilized. It felt like that ride at the county fair that spins so quickly you are paralyzed, plastered to the side of the wall. All I could do was look straight ahead at the blonde girl who now materialized in front of me.

She too had been holding up a key, and we finally had the angle right. For the briefest second, I gazed into my own eyes. Yet not just two eyes, but what seemed like thousands. It was like looking into an infinity mirror, except I knew it was not my reflection that was gazing back. There were countless other Chases staring back with the same mission, integrity, and fire that burned within me. Not all the Chases in the multiverse were on this track or had a Taylor at their side, but there were enough who were following this path to reach critical mass.

We had all arrived at the same conclusion that if we joined forces across the thin lining between worlds in the throne room, the amount of energy released from our physical matter and antimatter coming into close proximity to one another would be extremely powerful. The keys were just the conductors.

Powerful was an understatement. The tidal wave of energy seemed to magnify between us, refusing to let us operate on the same plane. We were bound together and torn apart at the same time, all feeling content by the fact that we knew we had succeeded.

And then all was dark.

PART 2

CHAPTER 12

"She's stirring," someone said above me. I couldn't bring myself to open my eyes. I felt paralyzed, with the exception of my hand twitching involuntarily. That eased my fear that I was not dead at least.

"It will still be at least a day before she's able to talk," another voice said.

"But we haven't seen anyone thrash around like that after they've arrived before. I hope she's alright."

I didn't recognize any of these voices. The murmuring continued as I lost track of time.

"Miss, if you can hear me," a louder voice broke free, clearly audible above the others. "My name is Eli and you are safe. It might be some time before you regain feeling throughout your body, but this is perfectly normal. You may feel weakness and confusion, especially in regard to recent events." He coughed. "It's going to be okay though, I assure you. Disorientation at this stage is perfectly normal."

At first I tried to protest that I was fine, but when my voice didn't come and my body didn't move as I urged it to, I started to panic. Not that anyone would have been able to tell as my body lay still.

I tried to recall the past few hours. I remembered being at The Safe and some of the people who were with me, but it was so blurry. It was like my brain was in a fog and I had been disturbed from a very deep slumber. I remembered seeing versions of myself staring back at me, but I couldn't picture what "me" looked like. Fear flooded me.

The air was stuffy and thick in my lungs, and I became aware of the fact that I wasn't breathing on my own.

My heart rate quickened, and those in the room seemed to notice. "Miss, it's going to be okay," the voice reiterated calmly. Why didn't these people know who I was? I realized at that point that I couldn't recall my name either. Was I suffering from some sort of trauma-induced amnesia? If I was having thoughts about amnesia, did that negate the possibility of me having it?

"It's been a while since you opened your eyes, so I'm going to walk you through how to do it," said the voice. "I want you to try to relax and bring awareness to your vision. Don't think about your eyes, per se, but what exists beyond your eyelids. Your eyelids are thin, so thin that you can almost see through them. Your eyelids are just shades that you can use like a lever to pull up."

I tried to see through my eyelids, but I felt trapped. There was only darkness, and I felt powerless. "Pretend you are drawing curtains," the voice continued. "Use your mind to connect the dots. Draw up the curtains."

Mentally, I envisioned red stage curtains that I could yank up with a pulley. I focused my energy on pulling a chain to draw the curtains up. Slowly, my eyes started to open. I couldn't make anything out—just vague outlines of large shapes and muted colors. It was like I was living in a sepia-toned, unfocused photo.

"Your vision is currently underdeveloped," said the voice. "Don't be alarmed. Your rods and cones should be waking up, and you'll regain full range of vision shortly. Don't try to speak yet, either, for that would trouble you even more I fear."

I suddenly felt like a lab rat with a strong instinct to escape, but I was rooted to the spot. I didn't feel any restraints tying me down, but I knew I wouldn't be able to get up independently. What was my name?

Before long, shapes started to come into focus. As the outlines became sharper, so did the colors. Along with my vision, my other senses started to return. My hearing had been fine, but I realized that my sense of smell had been absent. I started to pick up on faint scents of pine and rust. I looked around and saw a diverse group standing around me.

They shared an expression of anticipation, but not much else. They ranged in ethnicity and age, from what looked like their late thirties to mid-fifties, with hair, skin, and eye colors spanning the full spectrum. They looked like a clean and well-maintained group of individuals at first glance, and their clothing was bland though functional.

"We recommend trying to recount your memories prior to those of the last few weeks. The memories at the end tend to become less crystalized and more driven by a heightened sense of awareness, as opposed to materialistic details that right now seem so important for you to recall." The same voice that had spoken before now came from a middle-aged woman with piercing blue eyes and long, wavy brown hair. I sensed an alpha presence emanating from her; she was clearly a leader here.

My lips felt glued together, but I was able to start moving my tongue. I forced my jaw to move and finally opened my mouth. My voice came out garbled and uneven. I tried to verbalize a question, but all that came out were some indistinct guttural noises.

"You'll figure out how to talk soon, I have no doubt," the woman continued. "I can tell you're a quick study. I know you have so many questions, and you'll get all the answers in due time. Just know that now you are awake, and for the first time in your life, you are entirely in control of your actions."

I peered down for the first time, and saw tubes weaving in and out of my body. It appeared as though fluids were both entering and exiting at various points, but I could feel nothing. Aside from the tubes, my skin looked pale and smooth, my muscles lean and my limbs long. At that moment, I wanted nothing more than to look at my face.

As if reading my mind, the woman answered, "You're not ready to see yourself. You don't need to be worried, but you do look quite different than how you'd remember. We all are quite a bit thinner and paler than we imagine ourselves, to say the least. Yet this is your true self, as you will soon come to understand."

There was nothing I could do but wait. I wasn't hungry or thirsty—the tubes seemed to be addressing those needs. The crowd soon dispersed with a few lingerers staring back at me. "We'll come back and check on you in a few hours, once you've had a bit more time," was the last thing I heard before drifting off to sleep.

When I woke again, I had regained some of my motor abilities. My eyes opened more easily, and I could wiggle my fingers and toes. My voice, though hoarse, had returned. I didn't know what my first question should be; I had so many.

There were only two people by my side when I awoke—an older man and the middle-aged woman with piercing blue eyes. "Eli, she's awake again," said the woman, tapping the man softly on the shoulder.

"Hello there," he said to me, smiling. I could

feel his warmth and calmness emanating from his body. He was a friend.

"Hello," I replied hoarsely.

"I'm sorry we haven't been able to give you more information yet," he said. "It's a lot to take in so we try to space it out and give you room to process."

"You haven't given me any information yet," I corrected.

He smiled again.

"Where do you think you are?" he asked.

"A hospital of some sort. I believe there was an accident and I ended up here."

"An accident, you say? No, it was quite the contrary, definitely not an accident. It was a sheer force of will and a comprehensive understanding of yourself and the world around you that brought you here."

I had no reply, so he continued, "You can only come here by choice. It might be a sub-conscious, barely perceptible choice, but a choice nonetheless. This place is reserved for those who have achieved their greatest sense of purpose. It's complicated, but that's the bottom line."

As I had no idea what he was talking about, I tried a simpler route.

"Why can't I remember my name?"

"You probably will soon," he said. "It's like if you were in a deep sleep, it is often hard to recall the details of your dream on command. But they may or may not come back to you with time."

"I'm sorry, are you suggesting that my life has been a dream?"

"No, not at all, just the closest comparison that you'd be familiar with to what we will reveal shortly. Now, when you are ready, you can get up and get comfortable. I recommend getting up slowly—start by moving your limbs while lying down and then gradually rise up to a seated position. The tubes have been removed so you can move at will. Lynne and I will be here in case you need assistance."

The other lady gave me an encouraging smile.

On the third day, I walked. My limbs continued to ache, but the aching dulled and moved to the background of my consciousness. Lynne and Eli checked in on me regularly; they were kind and seemed to genuinely care about my well-being. The others just seemed more curious than anything, but they started engaging more in conversation as the days dragged on. After a week, they let me leave "my room" and gave me a brief tour of the building.

My room was part of a larger, sterile building with many identical rooms and many identical hallways. It made me think of Communist accommodations that I had learned about in college

—which now felt like decades ago—but cleaner and more purposeful. The tiled floor was cool to the touch, and the stucco walls also helped to maintain a pleasant temperature. The furniture was primarily earthy tones, with lots of gadgets lining the walls that I didn't understand. It seemed to me like hospital equipment, but they kept telling me this wasn't a hospital. I didn't rule out the possibility that I had been registered at a mental health center, though, as I still couldn't recall my name.

I soon learned they called this building the "port of entry." They also told me I would not be staying here much longer, which also reassured me that my mental faculties were intact.

"Would you like to get lunch outside today? I can give you a walking tour of the area this afternoon," said Lynne one morning. Lynne was naturally beautiful beyond her blue eyes that I had first noticed. Her relaxed waves fell effortlessly down to the small of her back. Her skin was bronze, and I could see wrinkles beginning to form on her forehead. She couldn't have been more than forty-five, but there was a wisdom about her that suggested quite a few more decades of life experience. She had been stern yet kind to me from the moment I had woken up and had been far more patient with me than I had been with myself.

I nodded enthusiastically; I was definitely ready to explore. My hope was that my piecemeal memories would become connected and fluid once I had the opportunity to immerse my other senses in the world around me. She escorted me out of the building, and I inhaled deeply. My first breath of fresh air in what seemed like ages.

Almost immediately, a familiar smell hung in the air. There was a thick scent of fresh cut grass, layered with a strong aroma of jasmine. It reminded me of summers growing up, Haley and I lying out on my lawn reading trashy magazines and gossiping about our love lives. I could almost hear her taunting me with her favorite tagline, "Chase only cares about the chase!" Just like that, my name and a slew of accompanying memories came flooding back.

I looked at Lynne, stuck out my hand, and introduced myself. "I'm Chase," I said simply.

"Welcome back, Miss Silver." She winked.

"You knew my name the whole time?" I asked. "How? Why didn't you just tell me?" I tried my best to sound non-accusatory.

"It's important that you are able to recover your memories on your own, so you are not influenced by what we say. Memory is a fickle thing, as you'll soon come to learn during your orientation. That will begin tomorrow. Today I am just going to give you the literal lay of the land. Your name is one of the few things you arrive with."

We had walked about fifty unremarkable yards from the Port of Entry building. There were walking paths spanning every direction, with small boxy buildings lining some of the paths—

trees and foliage lining others. My initial reaction was that everything in sight seemed highly functional and aesthetically simple. I had no idea what it would be zoned as—I couldn't tell if it was residential, commercial, or a mix. As if reading the questions on my mind, Lynne began to narrate our tour.

"The outskirts here are for residents who like to keep to themselves and aren't too involved with community activities. After everyone arrives and goes through orientation like you will, they then have to choose where they want to live —and this is largely based on what their *occupation* will be." Lynne placed a weird emphasis on the word, like it didn't quite accurately describe what she was wanting to articulate. "Everyone is given a plot of land and the materials to create a home of their choosing."

We continued to walk and explore, with Lynne pointing out all the geographical points of interest. The buildings drew closer together and had a more urban feeling to them, though I couldn't place my finger on what was triggering me to feel that way. I found it odd that we hadn't encountered other people on our walk, but Lynne pointed out that it was the middle of the day and most folks were working.

When we were close to returning to the Port of Entry, I noticed an enormous orchard with an outline of a seemingly never-ending structure on the horizon behind it. I started to ask about it, but Lynne brushed me off—kindly but sternly —and simply said, "That's all for today," and returned me to my quarters.

CHAPTER 13

The next morning, I found myself being escorted back along the walking path to a nearby plain building that contained only a single large conference room, as far as I could tell. Hundreds of chairs lined the floor, with an elevated stage. The stage had a few chairs on it, and I imagined those chairs would be filled by speakers who would be leading the "orientation."

A few other people had already arrived and were scattered throughout the room. They all sat at least a few seats away from one another, indicating that no one knew each other. That, at least, was a relief.

I took a seat near the outer aisle, second row from the front. I caught the eye of some of the other attendees, who all looked equally bewildered—and some seemed friendlier than others. We waited for another fifteen minutes or so, but only two more people trickled in. There seemed to be eight of us total, with no apparent connection between us. There was an obviously wide age range, to start.

The man I recognized as Eli approached the stage.

"Welcome, newcomers," he boomed. "On behalf of our community, I am thrilled to be speaking to you all today. You are our latest cohort, and we understand that you have so many questions. I assure you they will all be answered in due time, but I'm taking this opportunity to hopefully address your most pressing concerns. If you'd take a minute to look around the room, these folks are your colleagues. You eight all arrived here within the last six weeks or so, and we do apologize that information has been somewhat limited during that time. We try our best here to streamline information and present it in a group setting like this, in part to alleviate the strain on our other residents. It could easily be a full-time job just explaining the circumstances that brought you here, and that is an excess we simply cannot afford at the moment.

"In case you don't remember, my name is Eli. You can think of me as one of the elders here at Kaliland." He emphasized the last word and opened up his arms widely. "Yes, Kaliland. That is the name of this place, your new home. You'll be learning all about her very soon, but I'd like to give you some initial context about her origin story.

"More than a century ago, many of your hometowns reached a point of no return. A pandemic ravaged the world as we knew it. We hit a breaking point; much of the world was in despair. You'll learn more about this during your initial history lessons, but the point I want to make is that options for leadership at the time were very bleak. They decided to put more trust in technology than they did in humans, and they were able to save many lives accordingly.

"They eventually created a world where people could prosper, but there was a large catch." He paused and looked around for dramatic effect. "That world was virtual, and they let AI-based algorithms run the show. You are here because you beat the algorithm. But, I don't want to overwhelm you all with details at the moment. For now, let's move on to discussing our way of life here in Kaliland."

Naturally, it was difficult to move past Eli's dramatic opening remarks, and I missed most of what came next. My mind raced, mulling over his words. What algorithm had I beaten? Was he talking about Sid? I had so many questions, but I tuned back in briefly for the "need to know" details.

The closest concept for Kaliland I could draw a comparison to based off my fleeting attention during the presentation was an Israeli Kibbutz. Kaliland promoted a communal lifestyle where everyone worked together in order to support the community. For the most part, everyone ate together and received the same provisions, but was able to choose their line of work from the list of necessary professions. It seemed like most people spoke English and came from the Western world when they arrived, so I was curious why a more official government structure hadn't been set up yet. Perhaps Eli was saving that for later, or maybe it was too early and Kaliland hadn't yet received enough residents to warrant a formal government.

There was no Q&A following the presentation. The eight of us were led to a smaller room outside of the auditorium that had snacks and beverages. No instructions were given, and no residents joined us. It was just the newbies, and it was very quiet. For the most part, everyone in the crew just looked shell-shocked.

I surprised myself by being the first one to speak. Turning to the immediate man on my left, I smiled and, with a slight eye roll, said, "Well, that was informative."

He chuckled and replied, "Yes, that answered all of my questions. I now know the meaning of life and have a robust understanding of what the hell happened a month ago, and why I am here."

I was only 95 percent sure he was being sarcastic. "I'm Chase."

He shook my hand. "Braden," he replied. "So, what's your story, Chase?"

I recounted as much as I could about the past year of my life. I told him about my job at The Safe, about Alec, about navigating parallel universes, and about taking down Sid.

As I relayed all this out loud, it sounded like the plot of a fantastical action film. My thoughts drifted to Alec, wondering where he was now, hoping he understood my message. More than anything that had happened in Kaliland so far, it was this moment that really shook me. Was any of that real? It felt more solid than a dream, but only just—like a memory from decades ago that was fading quickly.

Braden had also "lived" in California, but closer to Los Angeles. Outside of that factoid though, we didn't seem to have much in common. He had been a successful manager at a renowned talent agency, representing A-list actors and living that dream Hollywood lifestyle. Eighteen months ago, or so he thought, he'd decided to take a sabbatical to, as he described it, "Do that whole finding the meaning of life thing." I met his last statement with a heavy eye roll and reconsidered his previous tone that I had understood to be sarcasm.

But he continued, "I know, I know it's so cliché. But I had the opportunity to travel around the world, or what I thought was the world..." He paused for a moment, clearly as confused as I was. "Anyway, when I got to South America, I went on this retreat with a Shaman in Peru. He led me on a self-cleansing journey with this intensely powerful drug. I felt like I had been trapped in my mind for six months, only to find out upon waking up that it was six hours. It was such a wild experience. I questioned everything about myself: why I acted a certain way, did the things I did, chose the life I led. It was incredibly therapeutic, and I woke up with this path set before me that I knew would lead to some sort of conclusion or awakening, or I don't know what.

"So, I stayed with the Shaman and learned his ways. He taught me how to clear my mind on command, focus on whatever it was I wanted answers to. He helped me unlock so much of my mind. I even levitated once."

I looked at him skeptically. "How many of the drugs were you on at that point of levitation?"

He smiled. "Let's just say it might have only been a few inches, but in my head I was very high above the ground."

He was exactly the kind of person I would have sneered at in my old life, but there was something endearing about the way he was sharing his story. He was somehow both humble and confident, calm and content in his demeanor. I liked him.

"I was all about that meditative lifestyle, and I started coaching others on how to achieve inner peace," he said. "But it was never about rejecting materialism or anything like that. It was more about focusing on the individual, and how we're all different and require different motivations and stimuli to truly achieve our potential. It was so important to understand that we are all complex and need to comprehend those complexities and nuances to the highest degree. Are you familiar with Maslow's Hierarchy of Needs?"

"Vaguely," I replied. I remembered the principles from my Psychology 101 class.

"Well, it became my mission to help others reach self-actualization, the highest tier of the pyramid." Braden drifted off momentarily and then concluded, "And I think I became pretty good at it, and that's how I ended up here."

I listened to some of the other folks' stories, and I felt like I was on the cusp of understanding where we were and why we were here. It seemed like "achieving one's true potential" seemed to be a common thread among the group just before each of us "arrived."

CHAPTER 14

Braden and I left the building together and agreed to walk each other to class the next morning, like I was back in high school. It was immensely comforting to know that we were in whatever this was together. There was a small classroom with two long wooden tables with benches on either side. The eight students each took a seat, and Lynne walked in shortly after.

"Hello everyone," she began. "I've already had the pleasure of meeting each of you, and I believe you've had a chance to now meet your peers. We'll be getting to know each other much better in the coming weeks. As a reminder, I'm Lynne. I'm going to be teaching you history. You're going to have to take my word for a lot of this because we don't exactly have textbooks to reference. I'll start by picking up right where Eli left off. As he alluded to yesterday, the world in actuality was far from what you've experienced in your lives so far. Let's start by covering some of the basics. Who can tell me what year it is?"

A young woman with a pixie cut answered, "2122."

"Does anyone have another guess?" asked

Lynne.

We all shook our heads.

"It's actually 2170," she said. "I'll explain more in a moment, but for you to understand properly I need to go back one hundred and fifty years or so. As Eli said yesterday, a worldwide pandemic had posed a very serious threat to our society. Fears of contagion led to incredibly extreme results. It was a highly contagious respiratory disease, with a formidable mortality rate. They tried to develop vaccines, but it continued to mutate at unprecedented levels. No one was immune.

"It wasn't long before this threat was taken seriously on a global level, and there were all sorts of proposals made. Governments tried to quarantine their countries for months on end in order to prevent the spread of the virus. Businesses were forced to close, and people were locked away in their homes. The global economy tanked, with mankind forced to rebuild their lives in a new paradigm of isolation. The world was crumbling, while everyone who was able worked toward finding a solution.

"A coalition of scientists, entrepreneurs, and philanthropists banded together in search of any technology that could alleviate this widespread despair. One research team in America made significant progress in the realm of artificial intelligence when it came to modeling and predicting human behavioral patterns. They did this in order to predict what would happen under certain policy adjustments that would permit people to leave their homes. Their AI program was able to interpret and mimic societal responses with alarming accuracy.

"In order to make these models under-standable by non-scientists—namely politicians who would be reacting to these scenarios—they created an immersive experience, much like the virtual reality concept you're probably already familiar with. Their audience would enter these 'models' so that they could actually feel the impact. You can imagine how effective this was for swaying often emotionally-driven decision-makers.

"Say they ran a scenario where they lifted the quarantine for one day and allowed people to go outside and get together with their friends in public. The incubation period for the virus was roughly two weeks, so they could live through this day and fast forward through the next two weeks until they could see the result. What they saw would be a resurgence of cases with hospitals overrun and desperate for help. Then, the politi-cians would go back to the drawing board.

"This technology was truly remarkable, and influential. The US was suddenly able to accur-ately predict moves, results, and countermoves by other sovereign powers. They were able to use these models to manipulate the world into saving itself. What I mean by that is they were able to enforce draconian but effective policies and promote investment in this technology that could help.

"There was not a single solution to pacifying the effects of the virus, but a combination of innovative technological, policy, and behavioral changes carried out together on a grand scale. The AI-based virtual reality model allowed for these technologies and behavioral changes to co-exist and thrive together. For a time, it seemed like humanity had been saved. The spread of the virus had been contained, as humanity at large continued to practice a phenomenon called social distancing where physical contact was kept to an absolute minimum. While people were eventually allowed to leave their homes, they did so cautiously and avoided large gatherings. They increasingly relied on virtual interactions to gather and communicate.

"Now as I continue, I want you to remember this VR model. It moved out of the public spotlight, but the algorithm supporting it continued to gather data. It continued to learn everything about how people and societies function."

Lynne took a moment to grab a sip of water. What she was describing sounded a lot like Sid. Though the whole bit about a pandemic ravaging the Earth felt like a very quick overview of what should have at least been an entire semester's worth of studies. She started lecturing again.

"Now luckily, this pandemic was but a blip in history, so I'm not going to spend too much time on it. But it did lay the groundwork for what was to come and why we are here. Eli has a flare for the dramatic and likes to use this period to frame our story. But it is important to point out that society had largely normalized by the mid 2020s in this new virtual-centric world, and that is where our lesson really begins."

We took a quick lunch break. The food I'd eaten here so far had been very hit or miss. Today we had oats soaked in some sort of nut milk with granola and berries. It was surprisingly refreshing, and filling. I felt ready to return to our lessons after refueling and having a few minutes to digest everything Lynne had said so far, and trying to align it with what I had learned in my previous education.

I vaguely remembered hearing about pandemics throughout world history, but I couldn't recall learning anything about a pandemic serving as a forcing function for a paradigm shift where people only gathered online. I remembered watching a documentary about the black plague and a nursery rhyme related to having a "pocket full of posies" that spun out of it. But that was it. I thought back to my parallel universe adventures and wondered if this was somehow related. And then I considered Eli's opening remarks from orientation. While I didn't understand the full implications of what "beating the algorithm" meant, a surge of anger passed through me as I realized that I had been trapped. And now I wanted to know why, and I wanted to do something about it.

When we returned from lunch, Lynne was accompanied by another older gentleman I hadn't seen before. He had very kind eyes, and she introduced him as Roger, a psychologist. I initially assumed he was there to keep a pulse on the class in case any of us started to become overwhelmed and have mental breakdowns. That definitely seemed plausible and hardly a stretch considering the circumstances.

But actually, Roger was there as a teacher. Lynne said understanding a bit of psychology was just as important as understanding history at this point in our learnings.

Roger took the floor. "Hello, all. I feel very privileged to be standing here in front of you. You may not realize it yet, but you are quite an exceptional group in the truest sense of the word." He spoke slowly and methodically, but not in an annoying way. His words were soothing.

"Now I understand from Lynne that you've touched on the pandemic this morning. You're probably wondering why that is being followed up by a psychology lesson. Well we're going to be co-teaching together moving forward, so it's definitely not a normal introductory psych class, if any of you remember taking one of those.

"After the effects of the pandemic abated, the world was left in a beautiful state—literally and metaphorically. Because so much of the polluting businesses and human habits contributing to negative climate effects had stopped so abruptly, the air and oceans were cleaner than they had been in centuries.

"People were invigorated and had a renewed sense of caring for their planet, and they wanted to maximize their time on it after being shut inside for so long. They thrived outdoors, exploring and socializing on pristine beaches and within National Parks. It was an incredible time to be alive, and for reference, we're talking about the early 2030s. That decade is what we call the Moonshot Age, and I would give anything to have lived through it."

Roger proceeded to hand each of us a pair of clouded eyeglasses.

"When you put these on, they'll offer visual aids alongside the lecture. If you tap the right side of the frame, the lens will become less opaque with the imagery and allow you to see more of myself and the room in front of you," he explained.

The glasses sat comfortably on the bridge of my nose, and I was immediately immersed in breathtaking scenery. There were lovely florals that he referred to as a "super bloom," crystal clear ocean waters, rivers filled with salmon swimming happily upstream. Some of this looked familiar and not too far off from what I believed I had experienced in my own life, but there was a bit more depth that I couldn't quite put my finger on. Tapping gently on the side of the glasses, Roger came back into focus.

"Feel free to play around with these on your own," he said. "You won't have additional context but much of the imagery speaks for itself. We'll learn more about the golden age that followed tomorrow."

After class concluded, we were all invited for a picnic outside in the spirit of the learnings of the day. We had none of the beautiful amenities that had been depicted in the photos, but it was pleasant outside as we sat on a blanket in a little park. There were meats and cheeses, fruits and nuts. We played charades and got to know each other better. It was the most I'd laughed in what felt like ages.

Braden joined me on the blanket and seemed relaxed and very much at peace.

"How are you so calm right now?" I asked, genuinely curious. "Don't get me wrong, this is a great time. But I still have so many questions and anxieties around where we are and how we got here. The more we learn, the less I understand."

We both still had our glasses on, but at that point he removed his, rubbing the lenses with his t-shirt. He had a small indentation on the bridge of his nose, accompanied by a few perfectly imperfect freckles I was just now noticing. "I just feel like this, right now, is honest. There's no façade; we're learning the true history, the truth about humanity and what really happened. And the fun we're having on this beautiful evening is authentic. Even if we don't have all the answers yet, that is enough for me, for now."

I took Braden's words to heart, and indeed I was able to sleep better that night than I had in recent memory. I woke up refreshed, and ready for the revelations of the new day. I played around with the glasses a bit and found some beautiful imagery, genuinely wonderful visuals to behold. Every time I tapped the center, a new scene would appear. I wasn't sure how the controls worked beyond this simple "channel surfing," but it was fun nonetheless. My favorite was a dynamic image of the aurora borealis shimmering in pink and green hues above a snow-capped mountain.

Reluctantly, I took off the spectacles so I'd make it on time to Roger's lesson.

"Our lesson from yesterday is one of my favorites to teach," began Roger, shortly after I entered and took my seat. "I love watching all of your faces as I show you the photos of the natural beauty that emerged. The Moonshot Age, while fleeting, was the true golden era of humanity. That is also how the people felt during this time: they were aware, they were grateful, and they wanted to do everything possible to preserve it.

"There was a tangible contentment that existed among the people. Everything was aligning to make it so; social, environmental, and government structures had all reached their peak efficacy in solving the pandemic, so the world could experience a moment of peace and harmony. Lynne is going to take it from here for a bit now."

Lynne approached the center of the room, with a thin black card in her hand. "I want to start by saying there is no catch here. This was indeed a blissful time in our history, and I want to show you now how it was possible. If you could please put your glasses back on and tap the right side." She firmly pressed the card in her hand, and the imagery in our glasses synced to Lynne's narration.

"So, what do you think enabled that Moonshot Age?" she continued. "The timing was right, that had a lot to do with it. Mankind had never been so motivated to preserve their outdoor world, after having it abruptly taken away from them for so long. If you think about how clear the air is after a big storm, it was like that, multiplied by a thousand. Better air, better everything. It's important to underscore how large of a role new technology played during this time too.

"The glasses you're wearing are a remnant of that era. Apologies for the low-tech, but it's the best we've been able to scavenge. As I mentioned the other day, innovators were under the gun like never before. They created models and machines to solve so many problems, big and small. Alternative energy sources and electrically powered transportation thrived after people saw the power of a pollutant-free world. There was a general shift toward environmentally friendly behavior." Lynne paused.

News headlines scrolled across the lenses. There were robots handling, well, everything. It looked like every industry from food sourcing, distribution, and preparation to transportation to medicine was increasingly being handled autonomously.

Lynne narrated in the background. "At the same time, technology trends from the pandemic lingered. As humans were forced to stay home, most of the technologies developed during that time became increasingly handled by artificial intelligence; they did not require much human effort.

"The pandemic had some other positive consequences, too. As industries like food production and distribution became more efficient due to the power of AI, fewer people went hungry. There were fewer errors in precision medicine, and early diagnosis tests made significant progress. People were able to get increased access to personalized, preventative health and dietary supplements so that they lived longer, healthier lives. And this was made possible by incredible advances in machine learning and robotic process automation."

A headline that read "100 is the new 75" flashed across the screen as she continued.

"Of course, humans were still needed to oversee these processes, but unemployment sky-rocketed as more and more jobs were better handled by automation. This was coupled with the already high unemployment rates that resulted from the pandemic-induced worldwide economic meltdown.

"Yet the technologies and societal policies worked together so that this transition away from human work was fairly smooth. Fortunately, it was an era of technology-powered abundance, but it required a dramatic change in the regulatory environment. There was a move away from taxes that were required to support bureaucratic programs, and instead a shift toward universal basic income. This shift allowed the masses to have financial resources that enabled them to live incredibly comfortable lives. Even those with jobs didn't have to work more than ten to fifteen hours a week. There just wasn't manual work to be done."

The scene in front of me displayed a family home with four people plastered in front of a white wall. They all had visors covering their eyes and were drinking from straws in unison.

"You can see this typical family enjoying a family meal together. All the nutrients and entertainment needed were supported by the government-provided income," she said.

My thoughts wrestled back and forth. On one hand, I understood the immense value in having essential needs and even comforts provided for all members of society. But there was a dullness that permeated even through the lens of the glasses. I pitied the family I was looking at, even without concretely knowing why.

I raised my hand at that point. "Lynne, can you elaborate on the policy changes that enabled this? I don't understand how all these people could be financially stable without wages. And those people just look so...disconnected."

Lynne nodded in agreement. "Yes, I understand why that may be confusing. The AI-based technologies reached a point where they were able to produce goods and services at an exceptionally low cost. Thanks to immersive technology, the cost of living an extravagant lifestyle became available from what you might think of as minimum wage. And because of the job loss, government sustainability from income tax became an impossibility."

I continued to stare at that family drinking their meal together, completely oblivious to the world around them. *What were they looking at? Were they conversing with each other's virtual selves through the visor display? Or were they on separate planes?*

Lynne cleared her throat, and my attention snapped back to the class. "At the same time," she continued, "many of the previous government functions became altogether obsolete compared to the new technological capabilities available, so private companies began to take over those as well. This drove down the cost of running the government, so business taxes went toward a universal basic income that provided every person with a monthly check to use at their discretion.

"This income was enough to cover many wants and all needs, and most people spent their days in the company of the people they loved, doing whatever recreational activities they pleased. They still spent much of their time engrossed in virtual activities, but it was a life of leisure. Many would argue this was the most utopian era for humanity. But not all.

"There was still a massive gap between those who lived on the government-provided income, and those who were powering the businesses. I cannot begin to express the wealth that this small group of individuals contained. They could have bought entire countries, if they were for sale. Even though much of their business proceeds were already being given away, they were able to afford the finest luxuries and any whim you could imagine. And that didn't sit well with some."

The inequality issue certainly wasn't what was gnawing at me, but something was setting my skin on fire.

"Politicians pushed beyond business taxes and started regulating away profits for the 'general welfare of the people.' They took so much that the brilliant individuals powering our society all but gave up and left to go live on their private pristine beaches. And who can blame them? Their life's work had largely been taken from them.

"It was this fight for equality over excellence where our story, here, begins. I'll pick back up there tomorrow. Thanks, everyone."

Agitated, I walked out abruptly. My mind buzzed with all of the historical gaps in my knowledge that had just been filled. I had never seen or heard of a world like the one that Lynne and Roger had described.

Trying to understand my emotional swing, I considered what Lynne had just said. The population had spent most of their time engrossed in virtual reality, but they weren't confined to it. I realized that I wasn't angry; I was jealous.

Again, I thought of the parallel universes that I'd believed I'd walked through only weeks ago. Was that how my subconscious was trying to break through to the truth? Deep down, did I know that my reality was not in fact real? That was a surprisingly comforting thought, knowing that I had somehow outsmarted whatever world I was trapped in. Like I had beaten the game. I didn't yet understand the full scope of what I was being told, but I was starting to piece it together.

"I think it's more than that," Braden told me after I explained how I was feeling. He was really good at getting me to talk, and I enjoyed opening up to him. "You caught on that something wasn't right in the grand scheme of the world, and you set about trying to fix it. I think it's your actions that landed you here. It's one thing to doubt reality, and it's an entirely other endeavor to try to seek out a new one."

I decided to go on my first run that afternoon since being in Kaliland, finally ready to embrace my frail body. While I felt healthy, I was far from strong. I ran to the little park where we'd had our picnic, past our sleeping quarters, classroom, and auditorium, and farther down the main path through the community that I hadn't yet explored.

The houses started to appear closer together, and I saw a few people here and there, milling about in their driveways. I really wanted to talk to them and ask them about their own arrival stories—what brought them here and what they were doing now. It was just starting to dawn on me that this community was just that, a community, and there were functioning people living out their lives here. What did they do all day? What did the future of living here entail?

As I ran past them, I contrasted the beautiful images of the Moonshot Age in my mind with the blandness that surrounded me. Boxy homes, dirt paths, some grassy areas and trees, but not too much else. The surroundings were bleak, and the people didn't seem too thrilled either.

I wondered what kinds of life events they had here, what they celebrated. Did they get married? Have families? My mind briefly drifted to Braden. He was becoming increasingly attractive the more I got to know him, and I could see us being together, but was that because I hadn't encountered any other realistic dating options?

My thoughts shifted to Alec. Was what we'd had ever real? He had been so charismatic and I had fallen victim to his charm in the beginning, but that had proven to be short-lived. The spark between us was completely interlinked with introducing me to the truth about Sid, and once I accepted that truth, I saw that in retrospect, the spark fizzled. We had used each other. Had I ever had a relationship where that wasn't the case?

I fantasized about a relationship that had inherent value. A relationship that was real, that could stand on its own, with no purpose other than itself. I couldn't think of a scenario in my life where that had applied. My sister had been used to make me into an agent. Alec had been used to make me question that life as an agent. For all I knew, my friendship with Hayley had been designed to set me on my path with Alec. I despaired at this realization and focused my attention on what I could do to amend it.

The next day, Roger began the lesson.

"It's a terribly fascinating thing, what happened next to humanity. Everyone still had their basic needs met, but because everything had to be perfectly equal and so many innovators 'retired,' the world just became...immensely boring. The world was still wary of a possible return of the pandemic, and this combined with a need for absolute equality had severe consequences. Most of the beautiful outdoor parks and bodies of water became prohibited government-only areas due to a fear of crowds, so people could no longer enjoy the best of what nature had to offer."

Roped off parking lots and closure signs at trailheads appeared in our lenses. The emptiness was beautiful but saddening.

"Remember, only a handful of people worked, so continuing to incentivize people to contribute toward the progress of society proved difficult. Of course, there were scholarly types who continued to educate themselves, but most people spent the better parts of their day immersed in online entertainment in order to pass the time. This was also encouraged by the government that still wanted to prevent an outbreak resulting from public gatherings.

"If you recall the advanced virtual reality model from the first day of class—that's one technology that became increasingly popular once it was released to the general public. It was so much more than the VR they were used to. At first, people began playing with it because it was such a remarkable model of the real world. People could explore places they didn't have access to otherwise, like all of those parks that were now closed to the public. Every person on the planet could virtually go sailing on the Pacific or hike in the redwoods if that's what they wanted to do.

"This immersive virtual reality experience democratized access to everything, without worries of overcrowding. And the artificial intelligence powering this world just became better and better at anticipating people's wants and needs. This gave the engineers behind the model a big idea: What if they could create a fully immersive metaverse to give individuals a sustaining purpose in life?"

The hair on the back of my neck stood up as Roger spoke.

"The technology was basically ready; its objectives just needed to be altered accordingly," he said. "People were spending more and more time in the virtual world, and less in the real one. Granted, they could still interact with each other in the virtual world, and in most ways, it mirrored reality. Except people could pursue whatever adventures they wanted, with whomever they wanted. They weren't confined geographically, meaning they weren't locked into only growing up with their neighbors, and they weren't beholden to the norms of the society that they were born into. There was so much more choice available to help them become the types of people that they wanted to be."

Even with these far less sophisticated augmented-reality glasses, I saw the appeal. We could trick ourselves into thinking we were anywhere, if that's what our technologically-altered senses told us. That could enable us to pretty much do anything. And if we were the ones tricking ourselves, did that make it less of a trick and more of a truth?

"That doesn't sound so bad," commented Braden.

"At that point, it wasn't," Roger continued. "Because the key here is that it was all about *choice*. You could be in the virtual world and leave at any point. Though more and more people were choosing to spend the majority of their lives there. And then a decade later, a new government-approved product emerged that allowed you to live in the virtual world permanently, with no exit available."

There was some nervous coughing among our group. I could see the realization was hitting us one by one, with the pit of my stomach dropping a moment before I noticed Braden's eyes grow wide behind his now moderately opaque glasses.

"You'd sign a contract and enter into a capsule where your mind would still be one hundred percent active, but all of your physical needs would be handled through tubes and such."

My mind flashed to my literal awakening in Kaliland. Braden was examining his hands, like he had never quite seen them before. The veins bulged in his arms as he flexed, and I envisioned the tubes coursing through them. It enraged me, thinking about him dormant and dependent on tubes for so long. Roger's calm demeanor didn't help, and only angered me further. He either didn't notice or wasn't bothered by the collective discontent in the room and continued anyway.

"This solved so many problems for the leaders of the time: everyone could be truly equal in this virtual world and their physical needs would be much cheaper to fulfill than providing an ongoing basic income. There was no risk of a virus spreading, as health security in general became almost guaranteed due to the isolating nature of the capsule. It was a win-win, in their eyes. And the public seemed to be onboard, as many people began signing up voluntarily. Whole families would go in together.

"The algorithms powering this immersive reality were able to ensure comfort, safety, and even help many find their purpose in life. If you think about the jobs that your friends did in the past—was anyone doing manual labor? Did you know anyone who was unhappy in their work? Did you ever wonder how certain people afforded their lifestyle even though all they did was play all day?"

Roger was right. Sure, there were small conflicts that had occurred over time with my friends and colleagues. My mouth crept up in a half smile as I thought about Hayley complaining about a boy who didn't call her back in what seemed like a lifetime ago.

But I didn't know anyone who had truly overcome adversity.

"Much of the virtual world design that now surrounded the people was built on what was available in the 2020s, when the technology was first created and had the biggest input of data. They decided to reset the clock for this group of permanent residents, to before the pandemic. At a certain point though, there came a question of what to do with the next generation, and the next, until your generation."

Roger paused in order to better emphasize his next statement.

"By now, you all should be coming to terms with the fact that your existence was contained entirely within this virtual metaverse, and my hope is that this discussion will shed some light on how it came to be. An international coalition was formed, within the metaverse of course, to discuss the long-term solution for offspring. The idea of procreation had been a big source of debate for citizens and leaders alike. They wanted to sustain our population and have real familial ties. But what did that look like in actuality within the metaverse?

"People were only experiencing the electrical impulses associated with physical intimacy, not the actual act, so natural procreation was no longer viable. The next logical step was artificial insemination from the couples who envisioned themselves having a child. Although, you still needed a means of incubating these children during the gestation period."

My hand slid to my stomach. I had never expressly wanted kids, but I certainly wanted the option of having kids. Braden seemed to follow my train of thought and gave my shoulder a small squeeze.

"That technology actually wasn't too hard to develop. We soon had gestation pods, where all of you spent your first nine months of existence. At the point of birth, babies were cared for in what you might think of as an ICU newborn room—all by artificially intelligent robots. You stayed there until your senses had developed enough to be entered into the metaverse."

"That is totally insane," one of my peers exclaimed. "You're telling us that our entire existence, literally from when we could begin processing thoughts, has been limited to this fictional reality? I thought you were going to get to a point where we had been brainwashed or something. But our entire beings are false. We've had no choice in the lives we choose to lead."

My thoughts had been building toward a crescendo, but upon hearing that, I retreated into silent despair.

Lynne replied soothingly, "Yes, we understand what this realization is like, because we've all been there. It is an inconceivable lie. At the same time, I disagree about your notion of choice. The metaverse was designed so that individuals had the opportunity to realize their full potential, achieve self-actualization. They had the ability to do this without most socio-economic barriers that existed in the physical realm. Most people still didn't realize their full potential, and those who did, well, have ended up here."

CHAPTER 15

I tossed and turned in bed that night, my mind recalling different periods of my life and then consequently trying to decode them. It was like there was a certain password I needed in order to understand what was real. I was somewhat successful in calming myself down emotionally, but my mind was still firing in all directions.

Lynne sat beside me at breakfast the next morning. "You know, there's a reason we have Roger teach some of these lessons," she said, slowly sipping her coffee. "He's a psychologist, remember. I'm not saying he has all the answers, but he's really able to help you make sense of this whole thing."

I nodded, stabbing my fork in my too-runny scrambled eggs. There was one burning question that I had to get off my chest. "Do you remember your family? Were they *real*?"

"Yes, I remember my family well," said Lynne. "My parents were kind, loving history professors at a local university who cherished our family. It's a bit ironic now when I think about it. So much of their life's work was a lie, not unlike everyone else I suppose. But I know that their love for each other, for me, was real. They met in the metaverse, and brought me up in the metaverse, and for them, that was enough. I'm sure some of their students were just AIs though, planted there to help them improve their teachings."

"Any idea what happened to those who knew about it and entered the metaverse under contract? Could they still remember what they did and what their life was like before?"

"Well, I was going to get to that in today's lesson, but I'll give you a piece of it now. This is where it really started to get dicey. Part of the contract was that they could never speak of the existence of the physical world again, to anyone outside of an AI-based therapist. The AI knew there would be underlying concerns and wanted to provide an outlet for that initial generation to be able to discuss without risking the integrity of the metaverse."

I guess that made sense in the craziest way. They couldn't break the fantasy by discussing it with one another, so they had to discuss whatever was on their mind with the fantasy itself.

After giving me a moment to think it through, Lynne continued, "The problem was when individuals started breaking the contract and confiding in their spouses or others. Of course, nothing in the metaverse was totally private— the AI processed everything. That's when the metaverse started splintering. The system simply removed people when they broke contract or threatened the integrity of the metaverse. We're still not sure what 'removing' entailed, but it wasn't good. We think they removed people from their 'world' and placed them in a new one where there were no other humans, only AI that resembled the people of their previous world. But I'll get more into that later today. I need to go finish getting ready for class." I reeled upon realizing that I had indeed accessed those other worlds, and the other Chases must have been AIs of myself.

"Deep breathing always helps," said Lynne as my anxiety became obvious. She pointed me toward a signup board near the entryway, and I signed up for my first meditation class that morning. We hadn't been broadly mixing with the larger community much, but Lynne had started introducing us to events to get us better integrated and acquainted.

The guided meditation was held in the park where we'd had the picnic a few days back, and there were about fifteen people—all much older than myself—spread out on thin towels. I followed suit, observing my fellow residents of Kaliland. They looked normal, and especially peaceful in this setting. No one was talking or making eye contact, even though the meditation hadn't yet begun.

I sat there alone with my thoughts, trying to comprehend all that I had heard over the past few days. I tried to balance the concepts of equality versus free will, and the idea of what actually constituted achieving self-actualization. These were all questions I imagined I would've tackled theoretically if I had studied philosophy. But this was real, not theoretical.

Recalling my former life, I focused on the demeanor of most of the people I knew. In retrospect, everyone just seemed really happy. I had always considered myself a bit of an outlier, wanting more and finding myself in a role of massive responsibility at The Safe.

I had been under the impression I was working for the most prestigious intelligence organization on the most classified of projects, as a girl in her twenties. I'd had the opportunity to wear technology-driven disguises and travel through the multiverse. As a third-party observer, it was indeed still fantastical. I smiled at the thought of having such a high threshold for achieving my purpose.

My family backstory seemed very blurry though. I could hardly recall specific times I had spent with my parents, or with my sister before she passed away. This was gnawing at me, and I wondered if they were part of the AI construction. My sister had been such a core part of my "story" for arriving at The Safe and needing to find answers.

But what if even she had been a figment of the metaverse's imagination, intended to help me achieve my state of self-actualization? That's what Alec had told me in a sense, that she had been used as a pawn to help me on my predetermined path. But that wasn't real. Was she? Was *he*?

A man with a dark goatee that obscured his age approached the center of the circle and invited us all to begin a twenty-minute meditative journey with him. It felt like two hours.

My mind returned to thoughts of Alec, wondering where he was now. Did he exist outside of the metaverse, and if so, would he ever make it here? At first it alarmed me that I didn't know if he had been real. But the more I thought about it, petty as it was, I felt better about how I'd left things considering the strong possibility that he was an AI. My thoughts subconsciously shifted to Braden, and I committed to bringing him here next time, and perhaps having him help me with a few one on one practice sessions in the meantime.

I was eager to return to class and hear more about the AI's inventions within the metaverse. When we took our seats, Roger looked contemplative but assumed his teaching role as usual. "Let's start today off with any questions you have," he said.

Braden raised his hand. "What happens when you die in the metaverse?" That question certainly woke me up, and I marveled at Braden's frankness. It was quite endearing.

"Yes, I thought that might come up soon," Roger replied. "It's much harder to physically die when your mind is confined to the metaverse. So most people—98%—actually die of age-related causes because there are so few external threats. When you die in the metaverse, you die in real life. It's like dying in a dream; it's not an actual representation of what is happening to your body, but you die nonetheless. Most of the really tragic accidents that you heard about only involved fictional AIs, as these accidents were events designed to help progress someone's story."

I thought of my sister again as Roger continued, "But when your friend's grandmother, say, died in her sleep, she most likely did pass away at that time, and her body was most likely cremated shortly after by robots. Those robots also bring the escapists, like yourselves, here."

"What about dreaming in the metaverse?" I asked, hung up on his earlier comment about dying in dreams. "Could the metaverse control our dreams?" I was thinking about how much I'd appreciated sleep in my former life, and how much I'd relied on my dreams and subconscious to guide me—especially toward the end.

"No, our physical makeup still requires rest, and with rest comes REM sleep and dreaming. Your dreams were your own." That was comforting at least.

Someone else asked why we got sick in the metaverse still, and all Roger said was, "Perfection is a bore." He was clearly preoccupied, and I noticed Lynne give him a slight nod from the corner of the room.

"Apologies all, I'm going to have to cut our

class short today. There's been a disturbance," he said. "I have time to take a few questions, but then I need to be going. Class should resume as usual tomorrow."

"What's the disturbance, Roger?" someone asked from the back.

Roger hesitated. "We haven't really discussed this yet, but there are two different factions here in Kaliland. There are those—the majority—who are against the metaverse, and the minority who support its process. We primarily just have ongoing peaceful debates about the arguments for and against its existence, and theoretical ideas about what we could do about it. Apparently, it got out of hand this morning, so they are calling a town hall for all permanent residents. Unfortunately, as you haven't graduated yet, you can't participate directly. But you are welcome to attend as observers."

There was no question that we were all going to attend, this being our first real introduction to the rest of the community.

The group of us entered the auditorium where our orientation had taken place. Eli was back up on stage, and he was energized, tapping his feet in eagerness.

Our group took our seats in the back, and

the rest of the auditorium filled in. It was the most people I had seen here by far, maybe four hundred. I had my doubts that there were many other people here, but I saw that Lynne had been true to her word and that there was indeed a community. Again, I wondered what all of their backstories were, and what they did now.

Eli cleared his throat.

"Good evening, everyone, and thank you for coming on such short notice. Now, what I love about our community here is that we don't have to use too many internal safety measures because of how much we trust each other, based on the rigorous test that you all passed that allowed you to be here in the first place. That is why we do not have a need for a jail; it's why we can trust everyone to take care of themselves. So, this is a bit unprecedented and it is why we've called this meeting here tonight.

"Earlier this morning, a gentleman, who for the time being will remain anonymous, was seen trying to enter the premises from where we receive our residents. That facility borders one of our orchards, and Eric here was out picking fruit and saw him scaling a tree in what looked like an attempt to jump the gate into the facility. We don't know what his intentions are, but we are trying to find out and deciding what to do next. And we'd like to open it up to the floor."

I remembered that building beyond the orchard from my first walk here. It definitely looked foreboding.

"Where is he now?" one audience member called out.

"Bring him on stage to join the conversation. I'm sure he had his reasons, whatever they may be," another said.

"Well, that's the thing—we can't find him," said Eli, shifting a bit uncomfortably. "By the time Eric had alerted us and we were able to search for him, he had vanished, presumably into the facility."

Murmuring spread amongst the crowd. It seemed very evident that no one had ever vanished from Kaliland before.

Eli cleared his throat. "Again, we can assume he was trying to get into the facility, but we don't know why."

I mouthed to Braden next to me, "What is the facility?" He just shrugged.

The lady on my left was in my cohort, but I hadn't really spoken with her one on one yet. She leaned over and whispered in my ear, "It's where the AI incinerates our physical bodies after we die and are removed from their metaverse. It must be connected to where the bodies are contained during life, though, but no one has been able to get past that point. Frankly, I don't think anyone has really tried."

At that point, I realized I had never asked how I had come to arrive in Kaliland beyond what Lynne had told us. I had just imagined myself waking up in that hospital-like room within its borders. The lady—I thought her name was Jenn—seemed to guess where my mind had wandered and continued.

"As far as I understand, there are only two ways out of the facility and zero ways in. You're born inside. And they remove you when you die, or when you wake up like us. I heard that they send your body in on a gurney with all the tubes in place, and a name tag. And that the 'Port of Entry' was actually created by the robots to help us get our start."

"And whoever was 'the first' to wake up, they just decided to start a life for themselves right next door?" asked Braden, who had evidently been listening in.

"I don't know. I think so. I think that person came to some sort of agreement with the AI."

We had missed some of the conversation happening on stage, but it seemed like there was not going to be any action taken at this time. They were going to wait and see if the man returned and assume the best of intentions in the meantime.

It made sense to give him the benefit of the doubt. Those of us in the room had allegedly achieved the greatest level understanding of ourselves and the true world around us, after all. Yet everyone did still seem a bit on edge, despite the rational agreement they had arrived at.

The next few days passed by without incident. I continued to go to classes and the guided meditations and felt pretty comfortable with my day to day routine. Jenn, Braden, and I stayed close and I felt a very natural repertoire emerging between the three of us.

While coming to terms with our revisionist history was still a work in progress, we were collectively less anxious by the day. We started to learn more about how life had evolved here, and the different ideologies that had prevailed amongst the residents.

Frankly though, there wasn't much to do. We ate, we learned, we walked around, we chatted. We pondered the greater meaning of life, which I thought we were all supposed to have individually answered as the price of entry here. But there were still a lot of open questions.

"What if we could just go back in, and pretend like we had never left? Would you do it?" Braden asked Jenn and me over breakfast.

Jenn replied, "No, I don't think I could pretend. I think I'd need to tell people I became close with, which would risk my mysterious removal from the metaverse altogether. Not worth it."

"What about if we went in as a group, like just those of us who know the truth, and we'd stick together in our own little metaverse community?" I posed the question as I debated internally. I wondered whether or not we had a responsibility to help everyone else who was still trapped, and considered if informing them would actually be helping or hurting. Were we elitist to keep our knowledge contained, or benevolent in allowing society to continue in blissful ignorance?

"Hmm, but then it would actually just be us alone, together for the rest of our lives. I like you guys a lot, but not that much," Braden chimed in with a smile. "I like the people here. I'm not itching to leave them."

"Fair enough," replied Jenn with a shrug. "Chase and I will leave you behind."

Lynn walked by and let us know that the man who had "escaped" had returned. "He's in a meeting with Eli now," she said. We were all very eager to learn more about his whereabouts.

CHAPTER 16

We learned the escapee's name was Randall.

There were murmurs about Randall's motivation and potential repercussions, but nothing concrete from Eli or any other residents. Yet he actually visited our class one morning shortly after to "clear the air." We were learning about the decision-making process at Kaliland and the highly regarded concept of a true democracy. It seemed like an appropriate time to have a guest who had operated outside of the prescribed norms.

"Good morning, all," said Lynne in her normal cheery voice. "Meet our guest today. Randall has been a resident for three years and has been an active voice in our community since he arrived." Randall waved from the side of the room as Lynne introduced him. "I'll let him tell you more about what he's been up to, and he's also here to answer any questions. We want you to know that you are true members of our community and we are committed to being transparent. That's the only way this place works. Remember that. Without further ado, Randall, would you like to come up and take the reins?"

Randall was a fit man who looked to be in

his forties with wide green eyes and a dark complexion. It was a striking combination.

"Hello there, I really appreciate the opportunity to meet and speak with you all today. As Lynne mentioned, I've been here for about three years. And I've dedicated those years to my studies, as you are doing now. I wanted to know if there was a chance to learn more about the world from which we came—if there was a way to get information directly from the source...

"...I don't know if you've gotten to this yet in your lessons, but all of the 'history' you are learning now is passed on from the original people who 'woke up.' It's they're collective memories. I'm not saying it isn't true; in fact I'm very confident that it's the truest thing we've ever known. But there's still a degree of bias and uncertainty, and I wanted to see if we could broaden our knowledge. So, I left and returned to where we came, or rather, emerged from."

He was a fellow truth-seeker, and I liked him already. He scanned the room and caught my eye, smiling warmly. I returned his gaze, and silently indicated that I was engaged and supportive with a quick nod.

"I didn't mean to cause a disturbance. We'd been discussing this as a community for quite some time, about venturing beyond our gates. I had always intended to come back, but I did not want to come back empty-handed. And I didn't."

Braden sat up a little straighter at that.

"Lynne mentioned that you hadn't been to the orchard yet, but the fruit trees are actually there to help obscure the facility from our view. I want to emphasize that the folks here are not trying to hide anything from you though—they aren't trying to trap you here. It's just that they didn't want the daily reminder that we were so close to the facility. So I think most people have intentionally forgotten about it. But I wanted to learn more, so I walked out. I didn't scale any trees like they initially thought. There's actually a door that no one seemed to notice. I walked out the door, straight up to the facility, and just knocked."

He had us captivated; we were all sitting on the edge of our seats waiting to hear what happened next.

"I heard the door click and unlock, and I just opened it. Now, you can't really tell from the outside, but the facility's depth is inconceivably huge. I'm sure I only saw a small fraction of it when I walked inside, but you can't even begin to imagine how massive it is. I couldn't see much of what is contained within its depths, but I found my way to an 'access' point pretty quickly. There was no one else in sight, which was a bit eerie, but I never felt unsafe. It's difficult to describe, but I didn't feel unwelcome. There was pretty much only one path I could take, and it must have extended nearly half a mile before I reached another door.

"When I pulled it open, I initially felt like I

had entered NASA with their giant computer displays. Just lines of code spanning massive screens on all the walls. In front of me seemed to be a sea of what looked like empty CT scanners, if you remember those." Images of the throne room permeated my thoughts.

"And you still didn't see anyone by that point?" Braden interrupted.

"No, although I have a very high degree of certainty that 'they' were watching me. I don't think it was an accident that everything was unlocked. In fact, I'm pretty sure they guided me to this room like they were observing what I would do."

"That's creepy," someone else chimed in.

"I don't disagree, so I wasn't ready to fully commit and try out one of the machines. I think we can assume that they'll bring you back into the metaverse, but it's not something I wanted to risk alone.

"From there, I simply went back the way I came. No harm done. Now, the reason we're having this discussion is because there's an ongoing debate about whether we should explore this further as a community. I wanted you all to hear about my experience from me, first-hand. Now you're up to speed and ready to join the conversation in a meaningful way."

"Thank you, Randall. We appreciate you coming here," Lynne said with a smile. Turning to our class, she added, "Randall's right. You're not just up to speed on this situation, but you are very much up to speed on much of Kaliland and our history. We will still be continuing lessons, but I think this is a good time to transition to the 'what's next' piece for you in this new life. We try to slowly integrate you into the way of life here, which I'm sure has become obvious by now. I've noticed some of you trying out the meditation and fitness classes available, and soon we'll transition you into more permanent housing and work programs. There's a lot more available than what you've been exposed to so far. And one of these key activities is weekly voting."

Lynne proceeded to explain that once a week every resident would receive a ballot with all proposed measures for the week. They could range from a simple homeowner's association-type request to a more philosophical issue like this one. It was part of how they ensured a true democracy. One resident, one equal vote.

Since the issue at hand was a more controversial one, there was going to be another public forum this evening for a discussion on next steps. Eli moderated, as usual. He didn't have a title per se, but I think it was understood that if there were a "President of Kaliland," it would be him.

Randall's proposal was definitely a polarizing topic, and there weren't just two sides. The room bristled with excitement, with so many who wanted to share their opinions on the situation at hand.

"We should investigate going back in and see what our options are for re-assimilating if we wanted to," one person said to a fairly shocked room.

"Why would you want to go back? It's all a lie! Really, after everything we've worked for here, you want to go back?" another replied—he was the man who led the meditation group. "I'm happy with the status quo. We have a great system in place here. Why rock the boat?"

"What does Randall think after having spent time in the facility?" the first speaker said.

Everyone's eyes turned and found Randall in the front row. He walked to the center of the room.

"I've been here a longer time than some, shorter than many," he began. "But it's clear to me that we can't undo the path we've already taken. It was never my intent to investigate being able to re-immerse ourselves in the metaverse. What I would like to consider is going in and retrieving some of our loved ones. I don't understand why we need to wait for them to wake up on their own, when we can vouch for them. Especially our children. As their parents, we should know what's best."

I wanted to ask how they even knew their kids were real, but I thought even casting that shadow of doubt would do more harm than good. I had been young and unattached for all intents and purposes. But not everyone here was the same.

Many of them had families and loved ones they'd inadvertently left behind. That would definitely shake the system up, though.

"How could we do that in reality? Like go retrieve their physical bodies? The shock alone might kill them if they don't wake up naturally," Jenn spoke up.

"Yes, I've thought about that," said Randall. "That was one of the reasons I went to explore the facility. I don't think it would be easy for us to access the bodies, let alone wake them up safely. I did get the feeling that we'd be able to reenter the metaverse and help our loved ones wake up the same way we did. It would be tricky though."

That was a jarring thought—that we could actually reenter the world we had grown up in, knowing everything we now knew. Sure, Jenn, Braden and I had theorized about what that would be like, but that only further stirred my internal debate on the topic.

Without a doubt, I wanted to help restore freedom of choice to the world. I just wasn't sure that waking people up was the best way to go about that.

Luckily, I wasn't the only one thinking along these lines. Lynne spoke up next. "If we went back in and disrupted certain people's lives there, that would be disrupting the entire system. Who knows what the ripple effect could be for billions of people? And why do you think we wouldn't be forcibly removed by the metaverse for risking its integrity? Are we ready to take that on?" She was genuinely asking.

"The thing is," Randall replied, "I don't think we'd be able to actually do anything that would work against the system. I'm not saying we wouldn't be putting ourselves in danger, but I don't think we'd have the capability of causing the metaverse to implode or anything like that. I think that's why I was able to access the facility so easily."

Chewing on my lip, I thought about my journey at The Safe. In hindsight, my plan to take down Sid had been half-baked. I had indeed cracked the code on how to do it, but Alec and I only briefly speculated on any unintended consequences of our actions early on. Good thing the metaverse had factored that in for me.

Weirdly, I tried to put myself in the metaverse's shoes. Perhaps the AI powering the metaverse was trying to learn as much about us as we were trying to learn about it. If that was the case, what would that mean for us reentering? Randall had made a good point about the metaverse not allowing us to "blow up" the system. I knew that to be true considering how it let me destroy Sid, leaving the rest of the virtual world intact.

"Logically, that makes sense, Chase," Jenn

replied after considering my theory. "I'm just not confident that we wouldn't get stuck there. What if the metaverse decides it can learn more by holding us hostage?"

It was a fair point, and one that came up repeatedly over the next few days as the community continued to debate our collective course of action.

Ultimately, the group decided to form a coalition of residents who would attempt to reenter the metaverse, fully accepting the small but considerable risk of not being able to return. We had a formulated a plan, but it was by no means foolproof.

We'd go in pairs, with assignments to "rescue" other residents' designated loved ones. We decided we couldn't rescue our own people, because we were presumably dead in their eyes and didn't want to shake up that ground.

Braden and I volunteered to go together, and I could tell Jenn was hurt. I didn't know if it was more about being left out, or a shimmer of jealousy I had begun to notice every time she glanced back and forth between Braden and myself. She hugged us each goodbye, her embrace with Braden lingering awkwardly. Or perhaps that was my trace of jealousy that was starting to peek through.

We were assigned Eric's daughter, Alicia, who lived in Chicago alone. She met the needs of the "checklist" that our community had put together to decide who could be woken up. She wasn't entrenched in her community and didn't have a family of her own. She was hard-working and had made a beautiful life for herself. She was independent and lived a life of goodness and compassion. I immediately liked her based on her profile, and I was excited to meet her and, ideally, successfully reunite her with her father.

Randall would lead the expedition of sixteen people to the facility. We were each assigned to one or two people in the metaverse and the mission was to "wake them up" in one week—and get out. We were not going to have contact with other residents during the week, which was disconcerting. But at least Braden and I were going in together. My body stirred in excitement at the notion of being alone with him on the adventure, daunting as it was.

As far as getting back, that was the biggest unknown. Before the technology became completely immersive, visitors to the virtual world could simply utter an escape phrase that they had programmed ahead of time. We hoped that this would be the same case for us.

Our group departed for the orchard and Randall went over the plan again. "When we get to the equipment room—let's call it the entry point—

we'll all find an open machine. There are plenty. I believe this is what they are there for. They haven't been used in quite some time, but I think they are the original pods that allowed people to go in and out of the metaverse at their leisure. From everything I've read in Kaliland, it looks like it's fairly easy. You essentially strap yourself in so all of the sensors are attached along your body, and it will be obvious how to get started. Hopefully we'll be able to program our respective destinations and escape phrases at that point."

We arrived uneventfully, and like Randall had said, the facility was essentially open to the public. We didn't see anyone as we entered and walked through the long hallway to the room with the pods. It was cold and felt like someone had recently cranked up the air conditioning so it was overcompensating, blowing frigid air and humming loudly. The hallway was empty and spotless, and seemed to continue for eternity. Again, I was reminded of my journey within the depths of The Safe. Butterflies erupted in the pit of my stomach.

Braden noticed my change in behavior and placed his hand on the small of my back to comfort me. "Look, if we're not back in a week when we're supposed to be, Eli and the others will come and find us. They keep reminding us that the AI is not our enemy; it's just not explicitly our friend."

"I just can't help the sinking feeling that it's a trap," I said, biting my lip again. And with that

I stopped talking. We were committed now: we were coming for Alicia and had the opportunity to reunite her with her father. We had to see this through.

Randall was right; the machines did look like CT scanners. There were countless machines lined up in rows that stretched on as far as the eye could see. It was a vast sea of machines, and there was an eerie glow emanating from each of them. I supposed that meant they had power. We were instructed to all stand by a machine and enter the town that we were assigned to.

Braden and I stood behind adjacent machines and pressed what appeared to be the "on" button. A touch screen popped up next to the button with green text running across it. It looked like a standard login screen that I was familiar with from my time at The Safe. The prompt asked for a username and password.

I heard whispering around me, as I evidently wasn't the only one who didn't know what to enter. Randall was making the rounds, so I waited quietly even though my stomach was churning with nerves.

"How are you doing, Chase? Stuck on the login screen?" he asked. I nodded.

He hit the small "back" arrow that returned us to the home screen. Next to "login" there was an option to "login as guest." Text scrolled across the screen that said, "Some functionality may be limited. Please proceed." The prompt then requested the destination, and I entered "Chicago." I breathed an audible sigh of relief when it asked for the escape phrase. I entered "home," and gave a thumb's up to Braden. He returned my gesture, and smiled encouragingly.

Randall offered to help me get strapped in. I waved once more to Braden and then leapt up onto the machine. My heart pounded as Randall wrapped the sensors around my feet, torso, hands, and head. I was engulfed in blackness, and Randall squeezed my shoulder to let me know I was good to go.

CHAPTER 17

A few seconds later, everything turned white. I had no sense of depth, so I brought my hands close to my face to try to adjust my vision to the light. My hands were gray two-dimensional objects. I peered down at my flat body, and it was as if I was just chalk on the pavement. I could see the outline of every inch of my torso and legs, all the way down to my feet. But there was nothing in between the lines. It was the most bizarre sensation I had yet experienced, and that was saying something.

Before long I noticed another outline of a body close by. I assumed it was Braden and waved encouragingly. He waved back. I had no way of knowing if it was him though, or just a computer-generated image. After a minute, the world around us started to materialize. The white morphed into colors, and our bodies became our own again. I looked down and appeared to be on a gurney in a sterile hospital room. Braden was strapped to a gurney next to me. Something was immediately off though; it looked like the opacity of our figures was only at about 60 percent. Like we were ghosts.

Braden started to release the straps, and I did the same. At that point, I couldn't tell if I was actually physically moving my hands, or if my mind was just tricking me into thinking I was. I knew to expect a confusing sensation like this, but it was so much more peculiar in reality. Once I was free from the gurney, I stood up and stretched out.

"How are you feeling?" Braden asked me, now standing about a foot away.

"Fine, I suppose. But it seems like we're a bit translucent. Do you think that's normal?"

"I have no idea, but we'll figure it out soon enough. I've just gotten very used to being pale, I guess...shall we?" Braden walked toward a door that had appeared out of nowhere and opened it for me with feigned chivalry. I knew he just didn't want to go first.

The skyline of Chicago appeared in the distance. I could vaguely make out the "x's" running down the side of the Hancock building. This immediately felt like the world I had grown up in. Somehow it was familiar, even though I had only spent one weekend in this version of Chicago over a decade ago.

Braden motioned to a sign that identified a train station a quarter of a mile away. We began walking toward it, feeling a crisp wind beat against our faces as we moved along. It already felt so real.

When we reached the platform, an electronic sign indicated that a train would be arriving in three minutes. It didn't seem like there was an option to purchase a ticket, so we just waited in silence. Soon enough, a train approached. It looked like one of the same high-speed rails that I had used for my fictional commute to The Safe. As we boarded, it felt exactly the same. Most of the seats were empty, and the few passengers were staring intently at their laptop screens. No one smiled or said anything to us as we found an empty row.

"I used to ride a train like this every day to work," I told Braden. "It really feels identical. Some of the people even look vaguely familiar. I'm currently experiencing the strangest form of déjà vu, because it did happen in the past—in some ways."

"Maybe it's the same exactly-coded train, just repeated in cities all over the world," suggested Braden. That made sense and made me feel like we'd have an easier time here than I had initially anticipated.

When the train arrived at Union Station, Braden and I exited promptly. We knew where Alicia lived, but we didn't want to arrive so unexpectedly. We needed to figure out a plan for the next week. I remembered staying at The Avenue hotel when I had visited so many years before, and naturally navigated us toward one of the few landmarks I was familiar with. It was a gloriously crisp, sunny day, and the leaves had a golden hue as we walked through Millennium Park. I guessed it had to be late September or early October.

Our energy never wavered during our three-mile trek, which seemed unusual. As we walked into the lobby, a receptionist greeted us warmly. "Welcome to The Avenue. Can I have your reservation number?"

"We don't have a reservation; do you have any availability?" Braden replied. She asked how many nights we planned on staying, and Braden said six. I wondered how we would pay for this, but I realized that an unpaid invoice probably wouldn't follow us out of the metaverse. She handed us a bronzed key card and wished us a pleasant stay.

We went up to the room, washed up, and wondered how we'd get by for the next week. "We technically don't need to eat, or shower, or even use the facilities," he reminded me." The machines back in the real world were handling all of our essential needs, which was both alarming and comforting at the same time. In some ways I felt invincible, even as I had a lingering question about my ghostly complexion. None of these facts stopped us from ordering room service, however.

Braden waited for the hotel staff to bring up our elaborate brunch order, and I opted to take a luxurious bubble bath. I kept telling myself it wasn't real, but it felt incredibly soothing and relaxing nonetheless. When the smell of coffee and eggs wafted into the bathroom, I emerged and put on the fluffiest of robes waiting for me on a satin hanger.

How do I have such a powerful sense of smell here? I thought to myself and made a mental note to seek out the answer when we got back. For the time being, I basked in the aroma.

The thought of meeting Alicia and leaving these comforts behind so quickly was very unappealing. Randall had warned us that we might be tempted to prolong our visit and delay our mission, but I didn't think my mental state would be so quickly affected.

We ate in silence, savoring every bite of poached eggs benedict, croissants, and berries. Again, I questioned how I was able to taste these fictional food items, but I didn't care. When we finished, Braden was the first to mention that we should make a plan.

I nodded and looked up Alicia's address on the hotel-provided tablet. She worked only a mile from us at an e-learning center. According to her career profile, she managed the programming for middle school-aged children's online education. We saw a picture of her in the corner, a young twenty-something with auburn ringlets, a slender nose, and hazel eyes. She would be hard to miss.

We decided to just go see if we could find her first and do some reconnaissance, which I was very familiar with from The Safe. We did need cover stories though, which I was happy to provide. We would be a couple considering moving to the Windy City for my new prospective job, and we wanted to carefully evaluate the education opportunities for our seven-year-old son, Madison, before pulling the trigger. It was just a little bit satisfying to know some of what I had spent my entire life doing would come in handy.

Braden and I left the hotel and walked briskly to the e-learning center. The doors were open, and there was a clipboard at the front desk to sign ourselves in. There was an "antique" bookstore on the left that we walked toward to pass some time. We picked up some of the classics and spent an hour thumbing through our favorites. It stayed mostly empty, with the exception of the bookstore coffee bar barista. I would have loved to sit down with a cappuccino, but we still had no money.

The barista walked over to us and smiled. As if reading my mind, she said, "Anything I can get you two on the house? It's been really quiet today, and I would love to make myself useful."

I smiled. "A cappuccino would be lovely."

"I'm fine, but thanks," said Braden.

"You're no fun," I told him after the barista walked away.

"I'm trying not to get distracted," he replied, running his fingers through his hair.

We sat down on a couch facing the lobby, with one cappuccino and two books in hand.

We saw people walking in and out of the building, but it was another two hours before Alicia emerged. I nudged Braden in the ribs and we watched Alicia sign out for the day. Promptly exiting the bookstore, we followed her, leaving a safe distance between us. She stopped at the supermarket on the corner and we followed her in. I tried to smile at her in the cereal aisle, but it must have come off as creepy because she immediately turned and walked in the other direction.

I shrugged at Braden, who was waiting by the door to follow her out once she was done. Alicia checked out, looked at her phone, and rushed out of the store hurriedly. Did she know she was being followed?

Braden and I walked out, leaving even more distance between us and Alicia. Eventually, she got to her building and used a fob to gain entry. We could have darted in after her, but we didn't want to unnerve her. We decided to try again tomorrow, because now at least we knew where she lived. I also wasn't upset about having to go back to my fluffy robe and luxurious bed for a night.

The next day was Saturday, October 4th, according to the date on the tablet. We decided to visit early to catch her at home, it being the weekend and all.

When we arrived at the front door, we scrolled through the directory to find her unit number. We buzzed and a deep male voice unexpectedly answered.

"Hello?"

"Hi there, we're old friends of Alicia's and happened to be in the neighborhood. Is she available for a quick chat?"

Even as I said it, I realized it sounded unconvincing.

"Uh, we're in the middle of something," the guy said. "Can you come back later?"

"It will just take a minute. I'm not sure when we'll be by here again."

"Sorry I can't help you right now, but I can let Alicia know you stopped by." He hung up without getting our names, but I couldn't say I blamed him.

Braden turned to me and said, "That went well." I rolled my eyes and motioned over to a park bench nearby.

We waited for a few hours until Alicia emerged alongside a gentleman wearing sunglasses with jet-black hair and a pointed chin. Her auburn curls bounced next to him.

We got up from the bench and I called out, "Alicia! Wait, this will just take a minute!"

The man turned around first to look at us and then Alicia peered behind her. He whispered something to her and they kept walking.

We followed them into a coffee shop and I just decided to go for it. We sat down at their table while the man was reading the paper and Alicia was sipping her coffee. He looked up but didn't say anything. She didn't even flinch.

"Hi, so I know this is atypical, but we really just wanted to introduce ourselves. I'm Chase, and this is Braden. Our fathers knew each other a ways back and my dad has been asking for me to get in touch to see how you are doing. It's been quite some time since he made that request, but I figured better late than never." I smiled.

She stared at us blankly. The man put his arm around her and kissed the top of her head, not saying anything.

"Yeah, so we were just wondering if we could take you out to lunch sometime or something," said Braden. I nudged him, silently reminding him we didn't have any money to do so. "Or we could even just go for a walk?" he said lamely.

Still no response. Was she in shock?

"Excuse me, love," the man said to Alicia. She nodded and looked down at her mug, as the man got up and motioned for us to follow him toward the back.

When we did, he said, "You should stop following us. This is inappropriate. Alicia hasn't recovered from the tragedy of her father's death, and has trouble processing any mention of it. If you don't mind, please leave us alone. You can let your dad know that you checked up on her and she's doing great."

He left us there standing in the doorway.

"We should just regroup and figure out a

new strategy," said Braden, so I followed him outside the shop.

As we walked back to the hotel, I was distracted. I didn't even notice when I bumped into a mother pushing a stroller with a toddler in it.

"Oh my gosh, I'm so sorry, ma'am. Are you okay?" I apologized profusely but she didn't even blink and just continued pushing the stroller down the street.

"Okay, what is going on? First Alicia doesn't even acknowledge our presence, and now this?" I was starting to sweat. Something was very wrong. "Braden! I don't think the people can see us!"

"What are you talking about? We've talked to loads of people since being here," he replied calmly.

I started thinking about who we had communicated with. There was the hotel receptionist, the barista at the e-learning center, the hotel employee who had brought us room service. They were all in the service industry. Our interactions had been amicable but brief.

"What if all the people we have talked to aren't actually people? What if they are just AIs? What if there's a wall separating us and the real humans?"

Braden thought about this for a minute. "I think you could be right. But what about the guy who was with Alicia? We talked to him..."

The realization hit me in the gut. "He's an AI. She's dating an AI, maybe even married to him.

Woah, this is unsettling."

Seeing them together made me realize with certainty that Alec had indeed been an AI, and it unnerved me.

Braden and I were carefully navigating the border between friendship and something more, but our relationship already had a depth to it that Alec and I had never reached.

"I don't know how we can reach her, though, if there's this invisible wall between us and the other humans," said Braden, shaking his head. "The system has definitely guessed what we are trying to do by now, if it didn't already. I think we should go back."

"Okay, let's just sleep on it for one more night and see if we come up with any ideas. If not, we'll go back in the morning," I said.

There were still a few hours of daylight left, so we walked over to Lincoln Park Zoo. I loved animals, and we walked around watching the penguins and the chimps being so carefree. Again, Braden took my hand encouragingly as we wandered, and I grasped his in return. Of course, the animals were just computer code, but the setting lifted our spirits. "We'll figure it out," he said, tightening his grip. I still marveled at how real his grasp felt, and how it made my heart skip a beat.

My mind did wander as I thought of where all the other animals were during this time. I hadn't really seen any in Kaliland, so I imagined they had all taken back their land once humanity had retreated from it. That thought was oddly comforting in the midst of all this.

When we got back to the room, though, I started crying. It was all too much, being there and truly seeing the lie that my life had been. It was one thing to hear about it in class, and another to be back here. I wasn't crying because I was sad, or scared, but because I was emotionally overwhelmed.

Braden hugged me tightly, and the warmth that emanated from his body felt so genuine. He moved to kiss me, and for a moment I welcomed it. But I didn't want our first romantic moment to be a lie, so I pulled away.

"Our feelings are real," was all he said. I nodded and crawled in bed, my brain telling me I needed sleep. I wanted him to lie next to me but reminded myself of the fact that we were actually lying fifteen feet apart back in the real world.

The next morning I felt better. I think my mind and my heart just needed time to recoup. Braden seemed to understand, but he brought up the next question looming over our heads:

"Well, what should we do now?"

It took me a minute to respond but it became clear that we had two options.

"We can go back and discuss with the others

CHASING ACTUALITY

or try to break through this invisible shield somehow. We should try to match what we think the
others are doing. Maybe we can find them somehow? Lynne was closest to us, geographically, but
I'm not sure that matters in this virtual world.
She's by some lake a few towns to the south, but
we don't have exact coordinates. It might be easiest to find Randall, as he was going to a small ski resort called Sundance."

Braden nodded in agreement. "I bet we can
get a train to anywhere back at the station we
came from. Let's try that."

We cleared out of the hotel and made our
way back to the station, ignoring the faux receptionist's goodbyes as we exited.

It wasn't difficult to find a train to our destination, as a computer monitor by our initial
departure point asked us where we were going.
Again, a train was set to conveniently arrive in
three minutes. But when we boarded the train, we
both sensed something was off. We could feel the
train moving, but the scenery outside stayed stagnant. It was the oddest sensation.

Braden looked at me sharply, clearly beginning to panic. My heart started racing. Were we
trapped like I had feared?

I tried to get up from my seat but I was immobilized by the jarring movement of the train.
"Okay, let's try not to panic. What's our next
move?" I asked. Braden was also clearly trying to
stand up, but his attempts were futile.

"Now would be a great time for us to use our escape words," he said. "Chase, you first."

Closing my eyes and taking a deep breath, I clearly articulated "Home."

I opened my eyes, and Braden was still sitting in front of me, and we were still on the train. This was not good, and a familiar voice crept into the back of my mind saying, "I told you so."

"Braden, you try." He did. Nothing changed.

The whirring of the train continued for what seemed like hours, but the trees outside stayed still. The only change I noticed was that they were starting to lose their color.

Eventually the train slowed, but we were still rooted to our seats. When it stopped and the doors opened, we braced ourselves for the worst.

Lynne and her partner James appeared in the doorway, and we were momentarily relieved. But it was a moment too long, and while we both screamed out at her to stop, it was too late. They were already on board.

"Well, at least we're stuck here together," she said upon realizing our dismal situation. We compared notes, and they'd had a similar experience and timeline to us.

We lost track of time. More of our crew boarded the train. And when you had no human urges, time seemed to become relative.

Everyone cycled through as many escape words as they could think of, over and over again. Nothing worked, and no one could stand. All we could do was wait for the Kaliland residents to come rescue us.

After what could have been three hours or three days, I had an idea.

"What if we suffocated ourselves, intentionally?"

Braden looked alarmed.

"Hear me out," I said. "Maybe it's like in a dream. If you threaten your own life and get your adrenaline going, maybe that will wake you?"

"It's an interesting idea, but also you could just die. Lynne, didn't you or Roger say that? That if you die in the metaverse, you die in real life?"

"Well, yes," Lynne said, twisting her mouth. "But maybe you don't have to die. Maybe you just need to hold your breath long enough to trick your mind into thinking your body is having its air supply cut off."

"We're running out of options," James chimed in. "I'll try it."

"No, let me," Lynne beat him to the punch. She started exhaling, emptying her lungs. We all simultaneously held our breath, but more because we were waiting to see what would happen. She started struggling to hold her breath any longer, her body convulsing and her face turning blue. Eventually, she gasped for air.

While everyone was focused on Lynne, asking if she was okay, I decided to give it a shot. I constricted my throat, cutting off my air supply. I closed my eyes, directing my attention inward.

197

Keeping my throat closed, it took every ounce of will I could muster to not fill my lungs. My limbs tensed and an internal battle raged on quietly inside me. My consciousness started to slip, but I knew I had to stay awake in order to keep air out of my system. I reminded myself over and over again that despite how I felt, the air around me was not real, and therefore I didn't need it.

For a split second, everything was blown out in the brightest light. I briefly thought this was the light at the end of the tunnel, but then saw the outline of my body appear. In that moment, I took a breath of air, true air, and my real body exhaled in relief.

CHAPTER 18

When I was able to regain my breath and sit up, I tore the sensors off in a fury. I was confident Braden wouldn't be too far behind me, considering his experience in meditation.

There weren't other chairs to sit in and I didn't want to stay anywhere near the machines, so I awkwardly hovered in the hallway. A few hours passed, and when I got tired of standing, I sat down on the floor, hugging my knees to my chest. What was taking Braden and the others so long?

I thought about shaking him awake but wasn't sure if that would affect his mental state at all. Was there an emergency "off" button? I went back in and searched the machines, but there was no obvious release. I took stock and acknowledged that soon I would be in dire need of food and facilities, so I had no choice but to leave and come back.

As I was walking out, it dawned on me that maybe Braden didn't actually know I was gone. What if there was an avatar of me now being operated by an AI because of the metaverse's aversion to discontinuity? The thought made me shiver.

The long hallway extended in front of me,

and as I made my way back out the way we had come in, I couldn't help but notice another off-shoot back toward the entrance. My curiosity got the better of me, and I was able to stave off my hunger a little longer. I followed the offshoot and became more confident that it had not been there when we arrived. It curved around the wall we had entered from and opened up into a broad room that had not been visible from our angle earlier.

There were a series of machines working along an assembly line. It looked like one long conveyor belt that was mostly empty. A gurney was being ushered along the conveyor belt and out of the building. I didn't know if the person inside was alive or dead, but it made sense that this was how the person would arrive and be shuttled to Kaliland. It was just another bizarre thing to see in person.

Curiosity overtook me, and I walked over to the conveyor belt and started to follow it back into the facility. Again, everything was completely open—there were no locks or security of any kind. The conveyor belt disappeared into an upward-facing chute that I couldn't access. But below the chute, oddly, appeared a house. It was a wooden cabin standing in the middle of this giant warehouse room that felt incredibly out of place.

The lights were on.

As I approached the front door, I felt compelled to knock. I didn't know what to expect, or why I was knocking, but I was certainly surprised when the door swung open and I was greeted by a very plain-looking sixty-year-old woman. She had silvery hair pulled back into a ponytail, and severely angled cheekbones. Her skin was smooth, so maybe her hair had distorted my immediate impression of her age.

She smiled. "Hello, Miss Silver. Do come in. Would you like some tea? English Breakfast, Rooibos, or Chamomile? Apologies, as my tea supply has been dwindling and I only have limited options."

"English Breakfast is fine," I said, as if this was the most normal interaction in the world. I followed her inside and stared. "Who are you?"

"Well, that's a very good question and we'll get there." She motioned for me to sit down on a crunchy leather couch. "But first let's address who you are. You have escaped the metaverse twice now. That's a first."

I didn't know what to say to that, so I sat in silence as she prepared the tea. Moments later, she handed me a mug and sat down across from me. Her voice was silky, and the more I looked at her face, the more intrigued I became.

"Don't misunderstand, I'm not upset at all. I'm impressed and have been eager to have this conversation with you. You must be famished too —would you like a sandwich?"

I nodded gratefully. Primal needs always had to be met first, no matter the circumstances. She returned to the kitchen and retrieved a plate of assorted meat and cheese sandwiches.

I dug in and let her continue speaking. "It's so very interesting. You're a bright girl, but not a genius in the strictest sense of the word. You're compassionate and kind, but not the most empathetic. You're determined, a natural leader. But still cautious, vulnerable, and modest. Defiant of unearned authority but willing to be open-minded, to listen, and to learn. Like I said, so interesting."

I could've easily been offended by any of those statements, but I wasn't. It seemed like more of a compliment, the fact that something about me had stumped her. "Whatever you are, you're exactly what is needed to progress and iterate. So, let's begin."

Finishing my third sandwich, I sat back in the chair and allowed my mind to focus. "What happened to Braden and the others? Are they okay? We were trapped. Why?"

She looked slightly annoyed by my outburst, but quickly regained her composure. "That is a default setting that kicks in when the integrity of the metaverse is threatened by an individual… or a group of individuals. It's sort of a limbo state that exists to prevent any tampering until someone is able to intervene. We haven't required that kind of intervention for a while, and I apologize for not being able to jump in immediately. It has only been an hour or so though since the train started running. I had no idea you'd all take such drastic actions so quickly...or that you'd be able to get out. Nothing is supposed to be able to happen to someone when they are in that state; that's the whole idea."

A pang of guilt washed over me. That hour had felt like a week. My feelings for Braden had intensified dramatically over the last seventy-two hours and the thought of leaving him there alone and in despair physically pained me. I composed myself, noting he was safe with the others for the time being, and that was most important.

"Okay," I said. "Can you release them now?"

"All in good time." My hands clenched in frustration, but she either didn't notice or didn't care. She continued without skipping a beat.

"Chase, please calm down. Your friends will be fine. I just want to have a few words with you first. My name is Lillian. I helped create this place many, many years ago. I'm one of the original co-founders and coders of the metaverse. Naturally, I had lots of help, but I've been here since day one. It's been more than one hundred and fifty years now since we envisioned this as an algorithm to study humanity and predict outcomes. Obviously, it's come a long way."

Dumbstruck, I saw no choice but to go along with her for the time being. "I have so many questions for you about the metaverse and how you developed it, but no offense, how are you still alive? And are you here by yourself?"

"It was always of the utmost importance to

have a human overseer for the algorithm, so part of our project was to ensure continuity on that front. Another one of my company's projects was developing a way for a person to upload their consciousness so that they could live forever.

"Now, this never proved to be a scalable endeavor, but we did patent the technology. Creating a human-like body that could harness a consciousness while not aging was the easy part. This is not my original body, but it is my original mind. Although admittedly, it is somewhat enhanced."

She explained a bit more about her existence, which I now presumed to be as close to immortal as anyone had ever come. I started rattling off more questions about her life's work.

"It is a great burden," she said. "But I am proud of what we have achieved. Allowing the world to prosper, giving the people what they want: free will, the greatest opportunity to achieve self-actualization, with all of the luxury life has to offer and none of the risk."

"But it's all a lie, isn't it?"

"It depends on how you define truth and reality. For everyone who has now been essentially born in the metaverse, that is the only reality they know. Their minds are able to do anything they would outside of the metaverse, and their bodies are just a vessel. They have so many more options, and the world is so much better off because of it. You haven't seen much from what I can tell, but all of the people of the world are now geographically contained to two percent of the total land mass. Nature has been restored, which was also part of my mandate."

"Are you saying this facility takes up two percent of the world?" It was a minor question, but I was curious. "Doesn't having everyone in the same place make all of humanity exceptionally vulnerable?"

"Well, we've selected the safest location in the world with the smallest likelihood of any natural disaster. In the event there is some sort of issue, every mile of the facility is independently protected. If you think about a spaceship, there are different air locks that can be activated so that if one section is compromised, it doesn't affect the whole. The same is true here, and the computers are backed up in each section. If anyone tried to blow this facility up, for example, the most damage they could do is to 100,000 people at a time. Even with a nuclear explosion."

"How many people are here? Has the metaverse evolved?" I wasn't sure what the right word was.

"There are about three billion humans contained here, plus those who reside outside of the metaverse next door in Kaliland. Geographically, this structure spans roughly the same square footage as that of Singapore, plus its vertical levels, if you remember your time there."

I thought of the floor scrapers as she continued.

"There may be pockets of other primitive communities in different areas of the planet, but I am very confident that 99 percent of people live within the metaverse. And the world and humanity have never thrived more." She peered at me, waiting for my next question.

"Don't you get lonely operating this by yourself?" I asked.

"At this point, there's not really much for me to do. I have enough checks in place that if anything goes awry, I'll know instantly. The most interesting thing to happen in a decade was watching you and your friends use the guest access portal. In terms of being lonely, no, that hasn't been an issue.

"One of my enhancements allows me to enter and exit the metaverse at will, and I essentially enter in god-mode every time. I have a wonderful life within the metaverse as well, and am able to live as many of those lives as I want. It's the most wonderful gift, even if it is also a burden.

"I also have my (AI)rmy here, as I like to fondly refer to them by. My squadron of AI-powered robots tends to humans' every need while they are here. They produce the nutrients, the medicine, and supplies necessary to keep bodies healthy and strong from birth until death. They oversee the gestation pods. They take care of cremation. They handle removing those who wake up..."

She cleared her throat, clearly wanting to

progress the conversation. "Now let's talk about why I've brought you here."

I realized at that moment that the cabin had only become visible to me because I had been invited.

"Chase, I've done my best to moderate this world and allow it to prosper to the fullest degree. And let me be clear, I'm only here to essentially supervise the code powering the AI. I don't have powers to control outright what happens within the metaverse. That would be far too much power for any individual."

"Are you able to shut everything down if there's an issue with the AI?" I asked.

"Not really. But because the AI is programmed to do what is best for humanity, that has never been an issue. If I were to simply 'power off' the metaverse, I believe most people would die of shock. Their bodies wouldn't be ready; they would be far weaker than you were when you exited. What would they all do? Where would they go? That's all of course theoretically based on a notion that the metaverse would no longer be necessary or preferred. There would have to be extensive preparation for a mass transition before any action could be taken."

She was right of course. We were talking about billions of people's lives that were fully being lived out within the metaverse.

"We're not here to talk about the ethics of the metaverse in absolute, binary terms, Chase." I nodded. "I brought you here because I'm curious about your perspective as someone who has lived unknowingly in the metaverse, and successfully emigrated from it to the physical world. You are the only one who truly understands at the most fundamental levels how this operates, as evidenced by the fact that you were able to use your mental faculties alone to exit the second time around. Only I have been able to do that up until now."

I took that as my cue to chime in. "Before we continue this conversation, could you please release my friends? The thought of them stuck there without being able to move, and especially the thought of Braden constantly worrying about me, it's unsettling to say the least."

"They're fine. None of them has the will power to truly hurt themselves." I wasn't altogether convinced, but I figured the sooner we chatted, the sooner I could work out how to rescue them.

"Can I ask you a few more questions?"

She nodded.

"Is there a connection between my work at The Safe and here? I can't quite articulate it, but I feel like they are linked."

She proceeded to explain to me the metaverse was designed to be able to offer people what they desired by reading their subconscious. The machine couldn't control the subconscious, but it could interpret it, and use that information to lay out a fulfilling life.

"Your subconscious questioned the nature of your reality, and in doing so, it unlocked a path that led you to a way of understanding an abstract, metaphorical version of the truth without compromising the integrity of the metaverse. It was the first time I saw that happen. Much of your journey was a manifestation of you guessing the truth about the capabilities of artificial intelligence. Your interpretation of parallel universes was also a metaphor for the many worlds that the metaverse offers. They coexist in the same time and space—but are inaccessible for most. Except you."

It took me a while to wrap my head around that.

She continued, "Many of the employees at The Safe were real humans and had similar patterns to you in terms of your subconscious drive. But you went off the charts. Alec and the entire Infosec Unit were created by the AI to be introduced to you and you alone. I observed your journey and was most intrigued."

"Ah. You were the recruiter that Alec had mentioned—'L'—weren't you?"

She nodded as I continued piecing it all together. "Yes, I couldn't help but insert myself to nudge the scenario along and see what happened. Your decision to sacrifice yourself in an attempt to destroy Sid and thwart Taylor showed me how committed you are to your values, even unknowingly. That is when I first thought about bringing you here for a discussion. But I assumed by your nature that you would eventually be back, and that you would be better educated and equipped to discuss the circumstances with me. And so here we are."

"I don't know why I'm different," I said honestly.

She replied, "Neither do I. I don't mean this offensively in the least, but nothing about your DNA or mental development is exceptional. It's something in you that is more than your mind or body."

Not knowing what to say to that, I pivoted the conversation to my feelings on the metaverse.

"Okay, well my mind has been swinging like a pendulum about what is right, what is wrong, and what is real. But one thing I know for certain is that humans should know when they are interacting with an AI versus another human. I'm not passing judgment on anyone who chooses to befriend the AIs, or be more than friends with them... I'm just saying they should know who—or rather what—they are talking to."

"Why? What difference does it make, as long as the relationship is real?" she asked.

At first, I didn't have a good answer. She was right in some ways; it was about the relationship. Was it discriminatory to make the AIs disclose themselves as such?

"It's a manipulation though," I concluded.

"The AIs are programmed to feed off human actions. It's not an authentic, independent relationship. It's almost parasitic."

"You're implying that the AIs do not have their own consciousness," she said with a frown. "Yes, they are mostly programmed to be in the service industry and do the jobs that the humans do not want. But does that mean they should be treated as another class altogether? That they should have to label themselves as such?"

I thought about Alec, and the AI who was with Alicia. And I looked at Lillian, part human and part AI, who stood before me. Did they have independent minds outside of serving the greater purpose of the humans who had initially programmed them?

"The issue is the unknown. The lack of transparency," I said. "If humans knew they were living in this metaverse alongside AIs, it would not be an issue, I suppose. Because they would know about the possibility. Right now, everyone is in the dark, and that prevents them from making educated decisions."

Lillian said nothing.

"Do you still remove people when they do something that compromises the metaverse? Where do they go?" I asked, changing the subject again.

"It's not really necessary anymore, because no one still alive, except me, remembers life before the metaverse. This has allowed us to stop the branching—what you perceived as the parallel universes. I do admit though, that was an ethical dilemma that arose when we were deciding how to protect the integrity of the metaverse. But yes, we still have that capability."

For a fleeting moment, she looked drained. "It's getting late. Chase, would you be willing to stay here for another day or two and continue our conversation? You can leave at any time, but future circumstances will dictate if you are able to return. There's a spare bedroom if you'd like to stay."

This was my chance.

"I'd be happy to, but you need to release my friends," I said firmly. "They cannot do any damage to the metaverse in their current state, and I demand that they be permitted to exit un-scathed."

She sighed, clearly not thinking them important enough to be worth her while. But she nodded and excused herself.

When she returned, she had a tablet in her hand. It looked like security camera footage facing the orchard. I could see a line of people walking toward the trees. "What do they think happened to me?" I asked.

"I didn't give them any ideas. They could see that your body was no longer in its machine, so I imagine they assumed you left to find help."

Feeling an immense sense of relief, I followed Lillian's directions to the spare bedroom and could barely crawl into the bed before falling into a deep slumber.

CHAPTER 19

I arose the next morning from a room that had been styled with a cozy mountain aesthetic, with wooden bedposts and a quilted blanket strewn across the bed. It felt comfortable, and I was reluctant to face whatever reality confronted me next.

When I entered the kitchen, a full breakfast had been prepared. I had wondered if Lillian still required human sustenance. I didn't know if she needed it, but she sat and ate with me.

"It's wonderful you decided to stay, Chase, thank you."

I wanted to tell her it was due to my utter exhaustion and intense curiosity, but I refrained. The feeling of being overwhelmed had normalized by this point. I had gotten used to it and decided just to keep moving through the days with an open mind of what to expect.

"I've been thinking about our conversation last night and am wondering if you'd be interested in preparing a proposal of sorts," she said. "It would be great to see what you come up with in regard to alterations that should be made to the metaverse. My curiosity is getting the better of me."

I blinked at her in surprise. "Really? You're interested in reading what I have to say? Why?"

"Again, whether you realize it or not, you are the first person to bend the metaverse to your will and intentionally escape. They say you only use a fraction of your mind throughout your life, but to be able to do that—consciously or not—requires an immense amount of mental control and activation. So yes, I'm very interested in your perspective."

"Alright, I could use some quiet time to write, if that's okay."

She smiled, handed me the tablet from yesterday, and left the room. It had been ages since I had space to write freely.

Trying hard to focus my mind, I stared at a blank screen on the tablet in front of me and started to type. The words poured out of me for some time. It was like they had already been written in my subconscious and were just waiting for me to put pen to paper, figuratively speaking.

The more I wrote, the more I believed Lillian was right. The metaverse could not be shut down outright but could be improved iteratively. Humanity was so codependent on its existence at this point that ripping the power cord would only wreak havoc and devastation. I thought I came up with some measurable improvements though. The proposal began to feel like a thesis, and I spent hour after hour typing, only taking infrequent breaks for food, water, and to use the facilities. I felt like I was in control and focused for the first time in a long time.

Writing had always been the way for me to formalize my thoughts, and I believed I was making significant headway.

I lost track of time. I could have been working for hours or days, but it felt good. When I finally emerged, I felt proud to share my work, confident that what I had written would be a strong guide for the entire world to subscribe to. It was grandiose, and I still had no idea what gave me that right.

Lillian read it quickly. She digested all of my work in a matter of minutes.

"Very good," she said as if she were my high school teacher. "I've been thinking about implementing one of your main points for a while, actually."

"Which one?" I asked.

"It's a substantial change, but I do feel like humans should be given a choice on whether or not they want to live within the metaverse in order to truly enable a 'free will' model. So I wholeheartedly agree; they should know what the situation is. I think they should be made aware when they reach the age of legal adulthood, perhaps sixteen."

"I think it's eighteen," I chimed in.

She replied, "Their minds are able to mature a bit faster in the metaverse. It's a small alteration, but because their bodies are well cared for, they are able to speed through adolescence. If I may continue," she proceeded, "perhaps at the age of sixteen, all humans will be introduced to their existence within the metaverse. They will receive an education about the true history of the world, much like what you received outside in Kaliland."

I looked at her inquisitively. How did she know that?

"Remember, I've seen inside your friends' minds. Anytime someone enters the metaverse, I'm able to see all that has taken place beforehand."

I shivered.

"I know that you think I have too much power, but there are fail-safes built in so I cannot abuse that knowledge. As I was saying, at age sixteen they will be presented with all the knowledge of the true world around them. They will be given the option to stay or to be released. They can be released at any time they choose, but they cannot come back. It is a one-way ticket, if you will."

I thought about that for a moment. Yes, it would be incredibly disruptive to life in the metaverse if you had people fluttering in and out of it at will. Those who wanted to remain immersed in the metaverse should be able to do so without that constant interruption. I nodded.

"What about if their parents tell them beforehand? Will they be punished like before?"

"It wasn't punishment," she said sharply.

"And no, parents will have the right to talk to their children beforehand, but it will not be recommended."

We continued to discuss minor adjustments, and practicalities, but we were in agreement when it came to the main point: disclosure and choice.

"There will be a massive influx of new Kaliland residents," I said. "We need to prepare for them."

We decided to give Kaliland a year of lead-time. In one year's time, Lillian would introduce the residents of the metaverse to the existence of the world beyond. I asked her how she planned to communicate this en masse and without chaos erupting. She thought spreading the word organically would ease the shock, until this new education could be systematized. She planned to start with the young people, spreading knowledge through short anonymous internet videos that would ignite debates through their digital communication streams.

This video series would show the true history of the physical world, the development of the metaverse, and what life looked like outside of it. The videos would go viral, as would the debates about their origin. From there, the younger generation would involve their elders, and at that point the knowledge would gradually become more widely accepted.

Lillian forecasted that rallies and protests

would naturally spring up in response to those who wanted to gain access to the physical world and leave the metaverse behind. These activists would receive all the knowledge needed to advance their understanding. It would only be then, when there would be a comprehension of what had actually transpired in the world, that humans would be offered a choice to leave. This choice would not have an expiration date but would indeed be binding and irrevocable.

It seemed like as good a plan as any, and I opted to return to Kaliland to help prepare for the imminent spike in population growth. Before I left, though, Lillian said I too had a ticket back that didn't expire. She offered me an apprenticeship, with the main perks being "god mode" metaverse access and a unique chance to achieve immortality. I thanked her and laughed, and only later realized that she was only partially joking.

When I returned to Kaliland, I went straight to Eli and Randall to summon a town hall meeting. I was eager to see Braden, but our reunion would have to wait. Eli and Randall were initially thrilled and relieved to see me, and later chastised me for making them worry. It felt good to be back in my community.

That evening, I took the stage.

"Good evening, residents. It's so wonderful to be back amongst you all. As you know, our efforts to retrieve loved ones from the metaverse did not go as planned. We were unable to communicate with them, but all is not lost. I am delayed in my return because I have been working with the...system." I paused, remembering that I wanted to keep the knowledge of the existence of Lillian to myself for the time being.

"The system is going to be informing humankind about the existence of the metaverse in one year's time. Each individual will have a choice on whether to leave or not. Once they make that choice to leave, they will not be able to return to the metaverse.

The crowd murmured in response. Eli held his hand up from the side of the stage, commanding instant quiet. He waved for me to continue.

"It's easy to assume that we'll have an influx of new residents in twelve months, but we must not panic. Remember, everyone has families, friends, and communities built into their lives in the metaverse. Some will be quicker than others to leave, but it's hard to know how many will want to take that leap right away. We must prepare for expansion and get the processes in place to be able to better scale our community over the next year, nonetheless."

There was an onslaught of questions that Eli and Randall helped me field. It seemed like emotions were mixed in response to the news, but it was also the biggest announcement and paradigm shift that most had encountered since arriving in Kaliland. I understood it would take some time to digest, but hopefully not too much time. We didn't have much to spare.

I saw Braden in the crowd, beaming at me. I suddenly wanted nothing more than to get off the stage and jump into his arms. There would be time for that later, though.

CHAPTER 20

The year passed by quickly.

What Kaliland had achieved in twelve months was remarkable. We now had massive rice terrace fields that looked like they were preserved from the first millennia, alongside expansive lumber yards with machines quickly processing wood around the clock. Farmland stretched for miles, and we made sure to replant seedlings every day.

It turned out that our residents had incredibly diversified backgrounds from their time in the metaverse, which sure came in handy. There was such an abundance of knowledge and an accompanying variety of skill sets. We had the ability to scale food production, water purification, home development, and sanitation.

We had expanded our medical facilities, and our education capabilities. Residents were being asked to take on multiple jobs, and as we were all aware of the one-year deadline looming over our heads, everyone was happy to do their part and work hard for the newcomers' arrival.

Braden and I became romantically involved shortly after my return from the facility. I felt like our relationship had been sparked by our shared dramatic experience in the metaverse but had now been built on an honest and healthy foundation. Admittedly, Jenn was not thrilled about being the third wheel and while we stayed friends, we didn't see as much of her after that.

One evening, Braden and I were sitting in the park and there was a spark between us that felt like the calm before the storm. "It's remarkable how much we have achieved since arriving here, isn't it?" he asked.

"I wouldn't say this is a utopia by any stretch of the imagination," I said. "But yes, it is remarkable. We have the systems in place that we need to educate, feed, and house people as they come. I just hope it's enough."

"It's so much more than that, Chase. We've built a community. What existed before was a network of residents who did what they needed to in order to get by. It was fine, but it wasn't a close-knit community like it is today. Think of all the relationships you've built in the last year. Those connections are meaningful."

Braden was right, of course. I hadn't forged any truly close relationships until I returned from Lillian's, and the residents of Kaliland had been forced to unite like never before considering the circumstances. I was reminded of one of my first evenings back, when I was lying awake in bed, unable to sleep. "You're restless," Braden had said, tucking a piece of hair behind my ear. "What's on your mind?"

"I just can't help but feel like I'm missing something." My role upon my return had been to oversee the project management of the preparation efforts in their entirety. It was a massive undertaking.

"Chase, you're not carrying this burden alone anymore. You have me, you have your friends, and you have this entire community supporting you." He'd wrapped his arms around me, and I'd felt so at home listening to his heart beating steadily under his shirt. My muscles relaxed as I succumbed to his soothing words. He was right, and he was real.

Now that we had a solution to our problem of giving humans the choice to leave, we had to come together in order to make preparing for that reality as seamless as possible.

For the most part, residents had been respectful about my "need to know" proclamation. I couldn't tell them about Lillian because I felt obligated to protect her and the future of the metaverse. I was far from sure that no one would object to our plan and try to take the future of the metaverse into their own hands. So, I said there was not enough time to prepare as it was, and I wasn't going to waste any of it debating about the source of the information. And that had been that.

I had the opportunity to meet some exceptional leaders of different projects along the way, and I told Braden that I wanted to host a dinner to thank them for their amazing work over the past year. He loved the idea and helped me plan it for the following evening.

It wasn't anything lavish, but about thirty of us gathered around tables beautifully set with fruits, bread, cheese, and wine.

I cleared my throat and everyone raised their wine cups, as glass was in limited supply. "I'd like to make a quick toast to all of you here tonight who have forged a path for the next generation of Kaliland residents. There are so many unknowns facing us, but we are here together to create a freer life for all who seek it. Thank you for your long days and sleepless nights dedicated to getting us ready. The community is indebted to you, and personally I am eternally grateful to you for accepting my news a year ago so gracefully. I'd like to turn it over to Eli now to speak more about what is to come."

Eli stood and continued the accolades. He had noticeably aged in the last year, with now shock-white hair reaching his shoulders. His skin had weathered more from the sun, but he had still managed to be the leader that Kaliland needed him to be.

He concluded his remarks with an optimistic tone. "Let's think about everyone else on the planet who will begin to be exposed to the truth tomorrow. Our trust is that the metaverse will help ease them into it and they will be best equipped to make informed decisions. But it's going to be hard for them. Everyone who arrives here will choose truth and actuality over luxury and guaranteed prosperity. They will be leaving friends and family behind. We never had to make that choice, so let's give them the courtesy and respect that they deserve, and strive to make this community even stronger."

Everyone cheered, and after the meal and some drunken laughter from the wine, we all returned to get some sleep.

The next morning was anti-climactic. Everyone had been on the edge of their seat, waiting for an influx of people to immediately overflow the Port of Entry. But it didn't happen. No one came.

A day went by, and then a week, and still no one.

Two weeks later, we had our first arrival. But she came in the same way that we all had and woke up blissfully unaware of the circumstances at hand.

We worried that I had been misinformed and that knowledge about the metaverse had not been disseminated like I had been led to believe. Why had this newcomer not been made aware about the nature of her reality?

I decided that if a full month passed by without any progress, I would return to the facility to speak with Lillian and get some answers. I laughed to myself when I thought about how much we had scrambled, hoping for extra time to prepare Kaliland during the thick of our transition, and now we were complaining about having some extra breathing room.

On the twenty-eighth day, we had two arrivals. They arrived in stretchers like normal, but when they awoke, there was a light of understanding in their eyes. The first question the boy had was, "Where is Er...?" He could barely speak, but he motioned outside, presumably to the girl who had arrived with him across the hall. Perplexed, we brought her in.

The two had arrived together. That was definitely a first. Once we wheeled her in and they were within arm's reach, they never stopped holding hands. They looked to be about twenty-five-years old, pale like all of us when first left the facility. They were definitely the youngest people to come here, even though I was not that much older when I first arrived. But there was no way they could have both achieved self-actualization in their youth at the exact same time, together. We couldn't wait to ask them questions.

Unfortunately, we knew we'd have to wait at least forty-eight to seventy-two hours at a minimum until they had proper time for their bodies to adjust to their new physical environment.

News of their arrival swept through Kaliland and the excitement seemed to electrify the community. People started coming by just to get a glimpse of them through the window like they were celebrities. I had missed a lot of the excitement when our group had returned from the facility, but apparently it was a similar vibe at that point. Gossip was limited in this town, so they took advantage of what they could get.

On the third day, Eli, Lynne, and I were permitted in the room with the two of them. We asked if they knew where they were and what brought them here. Their names were Erin and Mike, and they didn't know where they were, just that they were somewhere real.

We knew this was it, but we still had a hard time believing what we were hearing.

Erin spoke first. "We saw this video that had made its way around our friend group. Most people thought it was crazy, but Mike and I were intrigued. We watched it over and over again, listening to its revisionist history and how we were all contained within a metaverse, like a multiplayer video game. Except we hadn't been able to escape until now. It just really resonated with us. We wanted to get more people to understand that it was real, but still most of our crew laughed it off. I think they didn't want to think about the fact that their awesome lives might be a lie. They're just in denial. But not us!"

"Why do you think it resonated more with

the two of you?" Lynne asked.

Mike responded to her. "Well, you see, we're like vigilantes. We have always questioned authority and have all sorts of insider knowledge and we're always willing to question the truth that's presented to us. Our parents called us crazy, but we were right! They have to believe us now!"

The fact that our first residents to arrive were self-proclaimed conspiracy theorists wasn't altogether inspiring, but it was a start.

"Were you able to prove your theory of the metaverse? Did you try?" I asked.

Mike spoke up again. "Yeah, we did. We had this idea that all of the hospitality industry was robots. So we just started going to up random waiters in restaurants and asking if they were robots and they said yes!"

We looked at each other, puzzled, and conceded that was a clever move.

"How did you escape?" Eli seemed a bit annoyed as he asked, annoyed that the level of our collective intellect was going to dip. But we knew this was a small price to pay.

"In the video, they mentioned that any post office would be able to provide assistance in learning more or helping you transition out," said Erin. "So we envisioned, like, a secret entrance where you could get transported to the new world. We went to the post office and waited for someone to help us. They asked what they could do to help, and we said we wanted to learn more about the metaverse. Totally crazy, right? The lady who was helping us smiled and directed us into the room of safe deposit boxes. Then there was a secret back door that we went through that opened up into an atrium."

I smiled at Lillian's creativity on this one.

Erin continued, "When we went into the atrium, this man in a suave black suit came to greet us. He asked us if we'd watched the video and what we thought about it, and we said we were interested in going to the real world. He then droned on for a bit about what it meant to leave, and that we could never come back. He said we didn't have to make up our minds then and could come back whenever, but we were ready. And then he just led us through the other side of the atrium and there was this bright white light and then we woke up here," she finished breathlessly.

"That is so interesting." I meant it literally. "I'm curious, what did the two of you do for work in the metaverse?"

"Well, we actually had our own internet video channel where we followed claims that people had about the supernatural and the like," said Mike. "We proved and disproved their theories. It was quite popular."

I knew Lynne, Eli, and I were aligned in our thinking at that moment. We hoped that we were not about to have a whole group of eccentric conspiracy theorists as our incoming cohort of residents.

We kept glancing toward the door to receive news of additional arrivals, but then we realized that no one would actually know what became of Mike and Erin. It would take an enormous leap of faith to blindly follow them, which would be asking a lot from people we deemed to be followers of amateur conspiratorial reporters.

"Erin, did you do a video report on the metaverse and speculate on what leaving it would mean?"

"No, we didn't have a chance to yet," she said morosely. "We did share the video that we received but were still in the research phase when we got to the post office. And then we just wanted to go for it." So their followers were none the wiser.

"I bet they'll figure out what happened to us though," said Mike. "They'll be coming soon."

We didn't have any newcomers for another three months, which was quite a stretch even before the video was released. The next group who came was a family. In the metaverse, they lived on a farm in a remote northwestern town in the US. They decided to leave as a family simply because they came to the conclusion after discussing the video together that they wanted to see what it was like in the real world. They considered themselves pioneers.

Over the next few months, there was a slow trickle of adventurers, yogis, religious zealots—all of whom would be considered "extreme" in their respective fields. The video clearly hadn't been accepted on a mainstream level yet. We were waiting for the trickle to turn into a stream and then a river, but it just wasn't happening. That ended up being for the best, though, as we weren't quite as prepared as we initially thought we were.

There were gaps in our ability to quickly scale housing, so this gave us the opportunity to get more shelters in place. After nine months, we had our first recognizable visitor: Alicia.

I had retained my role as one of the initial interrogators upon arrival, for lack of a better word. I recognized Alicia as soon as I saw her and sent Braden to go find her father, Eric. She was overjoyed when she saw him and even though it was difficult for her to talk, I could see the emotions overwhelm the two of them.

"I knew there had to be more to your disappearance," she said after two days of recovery. "It didn't make any sense that you would leave on your own—you were healthy, happy, and seemed perfectly content. And they could never find a person with even the slightest motive to harm you. I knew it," she said again.

Apparently, the video was quite popular by this point and its origins had become a source of debate, as Lillian had predicted. Alicia said people were opening their minds to the idea of a world beyond but were much less ready to pull the trigger and leave. Unless they were really missing something in their lives, they were viewing this other world as an interesting theory. It was like they had received an invitation to enter a spaceship, but only so many actually wanted to travel to Mars when it came down to it.

"I suspect that if younger folks are able to convince their parents, they'll come," she said. "It's very difficult to break a familial bond. Although that is also the exact reason I came."

Her experience had been the same as the others: she had left through the post office's back door. We asked if she had said goodbye to her friends.

"I wrote them all letters explaining why I had to leave. I'm sure some of them still think I'm crazy and that I'm going on a wild goose hunt, but I bet some of them will consider following. It's a bit of a catch-22 because you want the best and brightest people to lead the charge, but they're also the ones with pretty comfortable lives in the metaverse."

"That's a really profound observation, love," said her father. I didn't know him well, but I could tell he was incredibly compassionate from the day he'd voiced his concern about Randall's disappearance.

"Yes, but our mission isn't to get everyone here. It's simply to give them a choice, to make them aware of their options," I said. They both nodded. It seemed like we were on track for achieving that mission. I just hoped it was enough.

We had a steady stream of new residents shortly after Alicia arrived. Their reasons for leaving the metaverse varied, but most of them had a tough time transitioning over their first few months. It was like they had come here expecting a grand adventure that would unveil to them all the deepest, darkest secrets of the universe. So initially, they were underwhelmed with Kaliland, and second-guessed their decision in leaving behind their creature comforts in the metaverse.

After that first phase, and once they had a broader understanding of the true history of our world and what real relationships could feel like, they seemed to at least come to terms with their decision, if they weren't altogether confident in it. It was an interesting psychological experiment, and Roger was taking careful notes. Those residents who arrived in pairs or groups were faring better than those who arrived solo. But we were constantly learning and making adjustments to our onboarding plan to make the transition as smooth as possible for everyone.

There came a time when we needed to decide on a formal constitution of governance, in addition to considering how to break up Kaliland into multiple entities. It had become too large and unruly to continue serving all of the residents in a unified fashion. There was talk of breaking up the existing community and expanding outward into separate sovereign communities. Our great debates continued in their traditional form, but it became clear that we were reaching a point when our true democracy would no longer be sustainable.

I naturally distanced myself from these discussions. I was not interested in politics nor the theoretical ramifications that different governing structures would have on our society. It seemed like no matter what we did, we had a historical reference to point to that would indicate success or failure, depending on the political inclination of the speaker. My theory of governance was simple: stay transparent and keep everyone informed —and leave everyone to their own devices except when it was paramount for public safety to mandate otherwise.

Braden found himself increasingly engaged in these talks and made it clear that he wanted to lead one of these new sovereign entities. I supported him but had no interest in joining.

One morning over breakfast, he asked me what I wanted to do with my life. I could tell he wasn't annoyed or trying to provoke me; he was just honestly asking. "You're one of the heroes here, Chase. You can do anything you want, but it's clear that you need to be a leader. Everyone here looks up to you."

Something about his comment triggered me and I felt shaken. I had the same intense feeling that I'd had the night before going after Sid. I had resigned myself to fulfilling a mission, and I hadn't cared what happened to me after that.

Now, I needed to do something that could sustain my thirst for positive impact, long-term. I didn't want to continue with completing a never-ending series of "missions." I needed a sustainable path forward where every day built upon the last.

I looked at Braden long and hard. He was my true companion, the truest of my life so far, and I loved him. That made accepting what I had to do so much harder.

CHAPTER 21

It was my twenty-eighth birthday, and I had a feeling it would be my last in the traditional sense. Braden threw me a surprise party, which of course was not a surprise. But it was a sweet gesture, nonetheless. All of my favorite people had come together in the same place to wish me a wonderful year ahead.

I always did love birthdays, and this also seemed like an opportune time for one last grand celebration, again. The cake and the company were splendid. At the end of the evening, I hugged each person tightly, blaming my overly emotional display of heartfelt warmth and gratitude on the wine.

It's funny how history repeats itself, no matter where you are in this world, or otherwise. I fully accepted that humans, at our core, didn't need to rely on a physical realm to survive, thrive, and repeat. We were a remarkable species.

The next afternoon, I packed a picnic lunch and some pen and paper, and left for a long walk. I found a quiet, grassy area about two miles outside of town. I set up a blanket and sat down to write the letter I had been dreading.

Dear Braden,

This is a difficult letter to write, but in my heart I know this is what needs to be done. I never told you about my time in the cabin. You wanted to know how I was able to influence the course of the future of the metaverse, and I lied. I said it had already been written and I was simply the messenger. But that was not the case.

Please don't be angry. The reason I didn't say anything is that I feared there would be an uprising that would result out of fear of what I'm about to tell you. And if you have faith in me at all, you will keep this to yourself. But I couldn't move on without coming forward, because transparency is what I value most, outside of our relationship. I love you and trust you, and know that you will respect my wishes.

The day that I held my breath and left the metaverse by will, I exerted a quality of mankind that I still can't explain. But I was able to achieve this feat uniquely, and I'm eager to learn why. When I woke up that day, a part of the facility made itself visible to me. There was a wooden cabin with a woman inside, and yes I am aware that it sounds like I'm on a hallucinogenic. If it wasn't for the manifestation of the new wave of newcomers, I might have thought it was just that, a hallucination.

The woman in the cabin oversees the metaverse in its entirety. Granted, the AI runs itself, but she is there to make sure the AI doesn't go awry. She is one of the original creators of the metaverse, and she has been biologically altered to be able to enter and exit it at will. Her mind is intact, but her body is artificial. She is in many ways the embodiment of the metaverse, and represents the potential for humanity. She could very well live forever.

Her name is Lillian, and she is kind. She was interested in having an open discussion with me about the state of the metaverse, which is how we arrived at the solution of allowing billions of people within the metaverse the opportunity to choose their fate. It is only the tip of the iceberg, though, as there is so much more that can be done. There are thousands of discussions to be had, and thousands of potential solutions to be tried. It's a world of endless possibility, when it comes to creating the best opportunities for the future of man-

kind.

And it may take 10,000 years to get there, but I'm patient, and time is no longer material.

Eternally yours,

Chase

Braden and I had a lovely evening together that night, with the warmth of summer keeping us content outside for hours. I think, on a subconscious level, he guessed that I was saying goodbye, because he held me tighter than ever. It was a night I would always remember, and while the circumstances were similar, I slept much sounder than I had the night before I went after Sid. I woke before dawn feeling revitalized and refreshed.

I placed the letter on Braden's bedside table, kissed him on the forehead, and left for the cabin beyond the orchard, and the immortal adventure that lay ahead of me.

Made in the USA
Monee, IL
26 February 2021